Philip Ogley

Le Glitch

First published 2019 by Canapé Publishing, UK

ISBN: 978-1-69115878-2 (Paperback)

www.pjogley.com

For Stan Mellema

Who lives somewhere in this book

Chapter 1 - Crêpe

High up from his window Jean Marc saw a car coming along the road from the bypass. He picked up his binoculars and leaned forward in his chair to get a better view. Ford Galaxy he guessed. He could tell by its unfashionable curves glinting in the April sunshine. The overhanging trees reflecting in its huge sloped windscreen. The clumsy way it handled the tight bends leading up to the village.

Not that he was much of a car expert. God no! He didn't even own one, couldn't even drive. He just liked his little game: make and model in a couple of seconds even at a few kilometres. If nothing else it gave him something to do.

'Probably a 2.2 litre,' he murmured to himself when he saw the enormous roof rack with a load of junk on top. Then the two adults and child inside. 'A 1.6 would never make it up the hill. No chance.'

He smiled at the thought of a family driving through France on holiday and arriving at a place like Crêpe. Driving along the deserted main street peering out at the shut-up shops. Poor bastards.

He got up from his chair and went through to his lounge to monitor their progress as they entered the village. Past the old guesthouse, the shut-up bakery, and the church. Then they slowed. Then stopped. Then started again. And after a series of jerky motions as if the driver was still learning how to drive, turned right onto the Place de Crêpe and parked in front of the Town Hall at an angle.

Jean Marc felt a surge of happiness. Most visitors drove around the square a few times then left. Either the way they'd come, or towards Ventrèche eight kilometres away in the other direction. This family had actually stopped.

The driver's door opened and a man in his mid-to-late thirties, his bald patch shining in the sun like a fifty pence piece, stepped out of the car. He stretched his arms upwards towards the sky a few times, stiff from the drive, then stood staring at the village square mesmerised by the glittering white limestone slabs laid out in front of him like a chessboard.

'*Vous êtes perdu?*' Jean Marc called down, unable to resist watching him any longer without saying anything.

The man wheeled around and looked up to a first-floor window in the Town Hall. His French was poor but he understood the word *perdu* - lost.

'*Bonjour,*' the man exclaimed.

'*Bonjour,*' replied Jean Marc.

'Is this Ventrèche?'

'No,' Jean Marc replied in English. 'This is Crêpe. Just a moment, I'll come down.'

Two minutes later a smartly dressed man in his mid-sixties was walking purposefully out of the Town Hall. 'I'm Jean Marc Bulot, Mayor of Crêpe,' he said introducing himself, shaking the man's hand firmly.

'*Bonjour, enchanté!*' replied the man. 'Alex Cassidy. My wife Sandra.' He pointed to a woman in the car. 'And our son, Tim.'

'*Bonjour,*' the Mayor exclaimed enthusiastically to the boy in the back. 'How are you Tim? Good holiday?'

'We're lost,' replied the boy. 'But Dad won't admit it.'

'We're not lost,' Alex countered quickly. 'We're exploring the delights of rural France.'

Jean Marc laughed as though it was the funniest thing he had ever heard.

'We were looking for a place to sleep for the night,' Sandra declared brusquely.

'There was a hotel here,' answered the Mayor, 'but it closed down in the 70s.'

'The 70s?' she said, levering herself out of the front seat.

'I say hotel,' Jean Marc ploughed on. 'More a guesthouse for migrant workers. We had a coal mine here once. A group of Italian miners from The Abruzzi came to work it. After the mine closed one guy stayed and married, he's dead now. The rest went back to Italy.'

'Where was this guesthouse?' she asked looking uneasy.

'There.' Jean Marc wagged his finger towards a building to the left of the church. 'You passed it on the way in.'

The Cassidys looked over to a soot-streaked four-story townhouse complete with rusting iron shutters. A sign above the door read in faint blue lettering *Auberge de Crêpe.*

'Looks like a prison,' she said flatly.

'Funnily enough,' answered the Mayor. 'During the war it was.'

'Anyway,' cut in Alex worried they were offending the poor man. 'Thanks for your time, but we'd better be going. Get everyone fed and watered.'

The Mayor smiled. He'd never heard that expression before. He liked it. Very apt. 'But can I offer you anything?' he asked sensing a slight reluctance in Alex Cassidy to leave. 'We don't have a cafe here as such - not any more - but I'm sure our splendid village secretary Miss Murs can make you something. She loves making tea.'

'Err,' Alex stalled.

The Mayor was right. In another life Alex Cassidy would have loved to have hung about with this old duffer. Shared a bottle of Pineau, or whatever they drank round here, and talked about the mystery of French village life. Perennially deserted and yet so pristine you could eat your dinner off the square. The hedges neatly trimmed, the flowers blooming, the Town Hall painted. Even the Mayor himself, dressed in his espadrilles, white trousers and blue cotton shirt, was immaculately turned out. As though waiting for a fanfare that would never come. But dressed for the occasion just in case.

'Anything?' the Mayor pressed. 'A glass of wine? Milk?' He looked at the boy.

'We'd better go,' Sandra Cassidy cut in urgently, looking at her husband. 'Where was this other town?'

'Ventrèche,' confirmed Alex.

Jean Marc screwed up his face like he was about to throw it in the bin. 'There's nothing there either,' the Mayor yelped.

'Are you sure?' queried the boy looking at his phone. 'On Tourist Trader, it says there's a hotel, two restaurants, a cafe, a castle, a campground and a supermarket. Gives the town four out of five stars in fact.'

'*Impossible*!' the Mayor exploded. 'Must be a mistake.'

'It's not. *Regardez*!' And shoved the phone in the Mayor's face.

The Mayor squinted. He'd left his reading glasses in his flat. 'Oh yes,' he blindly acknowledged. 'But just out of curiosity, how many stars does Crêpe get on this Tourist thing?'

The boy tapped his phone with lightning speed precision. 'None,' he announced a second later. 'It doesn't even have a listing.'

'Bah,' exploded the Mayor. 'I wouldn't believe that nonsense.'

'But weirdly,' continued the boy. 'This village doesn't seem to be on the map either.'

'Don't be absurd boy,' Jean Marc yelled out momentarily losing his patience. 'Of course it's on the map. This village has been here since the Middle Ages.'

'But I can't see it,' complained the boy showing the Mayor his phone again.

The Mayor waved the phone away. 'Take it from me young man. Crêpe exists all right, I've lived here all my life.'

'Mm,' replied the boy with an air of calculated genius about him. 'Yes, I suppose you're right. Funny though.' He looked back into his phone. 'Must be a glitch or something,' he concluded, shaking the handset a few times.

'And I'll tell you what, there's nothing in Ventrèche either. I'd rather shoot myself than go there.' The Mayor mimicked putting a gun to his head. 'If you want to go somewhere, I'd go to Gigot back down the bypass, much nicer.'

'We're going to Ventrèche,' Sandra said defiantly getting back in the car.

Jean Marc sagged forward. The first visitors he'd had in months and there was absolutely nothing he could do to stop them leaving.

Alex Cassidy offered his hand to the Mayor. '*Au revoir Monsieur*,' he said politely.

Jean Marc took it. 'I'm sorry we couldn't be more accommodating.'

'Maybe you should get that guesthouse renovated,' suggested Sandra. 'Would make a nice B&B.'

The Mayor replied with a thin smile.

'Au revoir then,' she said. 'Say *au revoir* Tim.'

'*Au revoir*,' said the boy smiling at the Mayor.

'Goodbye,' said Jean Marc.

And with that they were gone. Leaving the Mayor to sag forward a few more millimetres. One day he would be back on all fours like the apes he'd come from. Crawling back to his armchair for another night of joyless TV.

Chapter 2 - Birthday

A few minutes after the Ford Galaxy had blasted off towards Ventrèche, Jean Marc heard a voice. For a second he thought it was the bronze statue of Jeanne d'Arc on horseback in the centre of the square. Or the horrible gargoyles on the church tower with their bulging eyes and long protruding snouts. Or even the two statues of the two long dead saints outside the church whose names no one knew.

But it wasn't. It was Francis Conda trudging out of his house on Rue de Plante on the far side of the square carrying his mandatory five o'clock bottle of beer.

'Who were you speaking to?' he yelled as he trudged across the square, the heels of his old army boots snapping on the limestone slabs.

'No one,' replied the Mayor.

'Must be someone; I heard a car and voices.'

'Doesn't matter. They've gone now.'

'Who were they?'

'A nice English family with other places to go.'

'Shame. The old place is pretty at this time of year.'

'That's what they said.' The Mayor jerked his hand up violently towards the road to Ventrèche and the long since departed Cassidys. 'This village really is the pits, Francis. You can't even get a cup of coffee here.'

'Miss Murs serves coffee.'

‘She doesn’t!’ the Mayor exploded shooting a pellet of spittle onto the white slabs. It evaporated instantly in the hot sunshine. ‘She wheels a trolley out whenever the tree surgeon comes to prune the plane trees around the square. A pot of cold coffee and a plate of broken biscuits is about as far as our coffee culture stretches to. It's pathetic!'

Francis took a swig of beer. 'Hot, isn't it?' he declared desperately trying to veer away from the Mayor's obsession with the failings of the village.

‘Why can’t we do anything right here, Francis,’ he continued. ‘Other villages do. Even that hellhole Plante has a jazz festival and fewer people live there than live here. What’s wrong with us, we’re living in the dark ages for God’s sake.’

'That's rubbish,’ countered Francis. ‘It’s not a Jazz Festival at all. It’s four or five old farts playing dull blues and a bit of ragtime. They advertise themselves as three different acts but really, it’s the same guys dressed up in different suits and hats. It’s crap I assure you; I’ve been.’

‘At least they have some ingenuity. All we have is a summer fete with Bernard Cle’s grandson Raymond playing fuck-knows-what-music.’

‘Rap.’

'What?

'Rap music. He plays rap music.'

‘Well it’s not Jacques Brel I can tell you that.’ He flicked his thick grey hair to one side with his hand impersonating the great Belgian crooner.

The two men stood in silence for a moment exhausted from the conversation. Long shallow breaths inflating and deflating their lungs like two old accordions playing their final tunes. The strong aroma of menthol sweets they both chewed incessantly while watching TV quiz shows - such was the tension - wafted over the empty square like cheap air freshener.

'Well anyway,' Francis finally said patting his old friend on the back. 'I didn't come out here to say hello. It's my birthday.'

'Good God! Is it? I'd totally forgotten. I must be losing my mind.'

'You must be seeing as it's the same day as yours.'

'I think I'm chronically depressed. I'm only sixty-seven but it feels as though life is slipping away before my very eyes and there's nothing I can do about it. The days, months, and years piling up like driftwood on a beach ready to be burnt. One evening I'll go to bed and wake up paralyzed, unable to move or breathe. Lying there waiting for death to cut me down with a long sweep of its scythe.

'I feel like that most mornings,' Francis joked. 'But by the time I've ratchetted myself off my bed and fixed a barrel of coffee, I'm ready for another day.'

'I don't know how you do it?

Francis drained his beer. 'You should try it. Makes the days go quicker, especially that dull period between five and eight in the evening. I hate that. Always feel I'm waiting around for something, but I'm never sure what.'

'I'm not a drinker, Francis. You know that. Hangovers kill me.'

'You get used to them.'

The Mayor was shaking his head. 'I've known you all my life and I've never seen you ill or without a smile. Sometimes I think something is seriously wrong with you, do you know that? From the outside you look like a total wreck - you drink, you smoke, you cough, you fart and you smell. And yet inside you have the attitude and behaviour of a child. As though the world is still up for grabs and you can still conquer it. Even though you've hardly ever left this damn stupid village just like me. Most people would have shot themselves by now.'

'I've thought about it. Don't worry.'

'I don't even know if you're human,' said the Mayor bringing his pale, clean-shaven face to within a fist's width of his friend's grizzled mug. 'You never seem to suffer!'

Francis grinned and patted his friend on the shoulder again. 'Do you know something?'

'No.'

'We have this same conversation every year. And every year we end up doing the same thing.'

'Which is?'

'We get drunk.'

The Mayor sighed. 'I know and I dread it every time.'

'Your place or mine?' asked Francis rubbing his long beard, as black as the soot that used to cover it when he worked down the mine.

'Does it matter?'

'Of course it matters,' Francis boomed. 'It's of great importance. You know I like ritual and routine. It keeps me going.'

'I think it was mine last year,' said Jean Marc wearily.

'My place it is then,' Francis confirmed excitedly.

And with that they trotted off across the *Place de Crêpe*, across the *Rue De Plante* and into Francis' house. The only noise remaining was the sound of Jeanne d'Arc's horse tiptoeing across the limestone stabs towards the village gates and freedom.

Chapter 3 - The Talbot Auto Sleeper

It had gone four o'clock by the time Jean Marc finally rolled out of bed. He still had a thumping headache from Francis' killer-strong red Ventoux. But the intense nausea of the morning had gone. Now he was simply tired.

He took a sip of coffee, his fourth, and looked out of the window towards the bypass. Since being elected Mayor over ten years ago he'd often wondered how long he'd spent gazing out of the kitchen window.

When the old mayor, Maurice Lafarge, died and the position became available, Jean Marc could think of nothing worse. The role held no allure at all. Crêpe was already on a downward spiral and he didn't fancy being the one to take the flak when it hit rock bottom. Plus, the thought of putting in long hours paying lip service to prattling residents for little or no money, seemed like more of a prison sentence than a job.

Until Francis reminded him one Saturday lunchtime at Jean Marc's old house near the crumbling stadium after their weekly 'banquet' of tinned *Confit du Canard*, oven chips and strawberry ice cream. 'If I remember correctly it comes with a free apartment above the Town Hall, plus free internet and phone calls. Even photocopying,' he added urgently as though free photocopying was of supreme importance to a retired man in his mid-sixties.

'Really?' rallied Jean Marc. 'I never knew that.'

'Oh yeah,' confirmed Francis pouring himself a huge glass of Pineau and settling in front of the fire. 'As much as you want. And the apartment isn't bad either. I've heard it's quite plush. And the view's better than that overgrown football field you've got out there.' Francis pointed outside to the mass of thistle and cow parsley. 'You could hide an army in there.'

'Maybe you're right,' concluded Jean Marc joining his friend with a mug of mint tea - he rarely drank alcohol even on a Saturday. 'You'd better nominate me then - no one else will.'

When the mayoral results came in a few months later, there was no celebration. The result was a given. No one else had put themselves forward and no one else was nominated. Jean Marc Bulot was officially crowned, by twenty-four votes to one, the 65th Mayor of Crêpe. The only vote against him was of course his old friend Francis Conda.

'To make sure all the votes were counted,' the drunk had triumphantly declared. 'Check democracy is still working.'

Jean Marc smiled at the memory and was about to go and make another cup of coffee and swallow another round of aspirin, maybe double the dose and go straight to bed, when he saw it.

'Bloody hell,' he whispered to himself as an off-white Talbot Autosleeper came over the brow of the hill and into the village. 'Haven't seen one of those for years.'

He tried to think of when. Five years ago perhaps, and that too was off-white. Or maybe it was just dirty. But he remembered it being weighed down with surfboards and bicycles. A GB sign, just visible through the spokes of a bicycle wheel hanging off the back.

It was unlikely to be the same one. Unless they lived here, or were delivering something, most people only visited Crêpe once.

He rushed down the rickety staircase and outside into the square, just as the vehicle pulled up in front of the Town Hall in the same place the Cassidys had parked the day before.

'Is this Crap?' the driver asked Jean Marc, bypassing such formalities as Hello or Good Evening.

'Bonsoir,' said Jean Marc politely. *'Oui. C'est Crêpe.'*

'Do you speak English?'

'Of course.'

'Good. I was in a village back there, can't remember its name, and they didn't speak a word. Could have been speaking Chinese for all I knew.'

'Well I speak perfect Chinese,' quipped Jean Marc.

But the joke was lost.

'I'd prefer English if you don't mind,' the man yawned. 'You see, we're looking for somewhere to eat. Fucking starving in fact - you got anywhere?'

And then the idea the 65th Mayor of Crêpe had been waiting for all his life hit him on the head like a piano falling from a thirty-story building.

'Oh my God!' exclaimed the Mayor.

'Are you OK. I'm not fussed. Kebab, burger, chips.'

'No no no,' the Mayor pleaded. 'I'm fine.'

'Good.' The man looked nervous, his hand was twitching near the ignition, ready to turn the key, start the engine and burn out of this hellhole as fast as possible.

'Our restaurant is currently closed for refurbishment,' continued the Mayor. He pointed to a derelict shop front, which in Crêpe's heyday was called Bar La Boucle. 'But I can give our chef a quick ring if you like.'

'What's happening Derek?' came a voice hidden under a pile of blankets in the back of the camper.

'Nothing Sheila,' the man spouted. 'Go back to sleep.'

'Had a few too many vinos last night,' the man gestured to Jean Marc. 'Still recovering. Ratarsed she was.'

'I'll give Madame Coquelicot a ring now and see what she can do,' pressed Jean Marc desperately not wanting to lose them.

He knew it might be a risk sending two English drunks over to a woman in her nineties. But then again, what did he have to lose? Plus, Madame Coquelicot was as tough as the steaks her husband Clement used to sell when he was the village butcher. Clement had died over ten years ago but she still kept a stash of meat in the giant freezer behind her house.

'She does an excellent steak-frites,' added the Mayor.

'Steak-frites!'

The head of Sheila (he presumed) appeared through the seats. A podgy-faced woman who looked like her husband, except redder.

'This is Sheila my wife. I'm Derek Palmer,' he introduced them both as they got out of the camper.

'E*nchanté*,' said Jean Marc.

'Yes,' said Derek, unsure of the correct response.

'Did you say steak-frites, I could have a go on that?' said Sheila like it was a fairground ride. 'Luv-it!'

'Steak-frites is her speciality,' offered Jean Marc. 'You wait here and I'll give her a ring.'

The Mayor returned five minutes later. 'She'll see you in five minutes. It's the house at the end of the village. Green door. She's expecting you.'

'We haven't got any cash on us,' panicked Sheila. 'Does she take cards?'

Jean Marc let out a short laugh. 'Don't worry, this one's on the village,' stated Jean Marc proudly. 'We're having a marketing drive.'

The couple gazed around at the desolation. 'As you can see,' the Mayor added quickly. 'We're just starting up - although we have had the square repaved.'

He was going to add nine years ago, but they didn't need to know that.

'It's very nice,' commented Sheila.

'We once had a post office. A bank, three bars, a butcher, two bakeries, a patisserie, two restaurants and a guest house.' He pointed to the row of broken-down shops on the right-hand side of the square. Even a hairdresser. Can you believe it?'

'Err, no.' Derek shook his head.

Jean Marc agreed. It was difficult to see how such a deserted place was once so lively. But he remembered the weekends when the three bars were full of drunken miners and on Saturday mornings the square was clogged with the comatose bodies of those who had failed to make it to the guesthouse two hundred metres away.

'Sign of the times,' sighed Sheila. 'Same back home.'

'Is it?' Jean Marc jumped to attention.

'Oh yes, our whole town is full of empty shops, bars and restaurants.'

'God, I never knew. I thought the UK was booming.'

'You should visit sometime, see for yourself,' commented Derek.

'Maybe I will,' said the Mayor weakly, thrusting his arm forward for a handshake. But they'd already turned their backs and were getting back into the camper.

'Anyway,' said Derek from the open window. 'Good luck and good to talk to you. End of the village you say?'

'You'll see the sign for Ventrèche,' offered the Mayor pretending to rub an itch on his hand to cover the embarrassment of the aborted handshake. 'It's just after that. You can't miss it. Green door the size of Wembley stadium.'

Derek smiled. 'Thanks for your help.'

'Seeya,' said Sheila.

And with that Jean Marc watched them drive off round the square, turn left onto the *Rue de Plante*, right at the crossroads and onto the road towards Ventrèche. As he walked up the old staircase to his flat, he felt light. Almost happy. Two cars in two days. He couldn't remember the last time that had happened.

Chapter 4 - Henry Clark

The 1974 census recorded 602 people living in Crêpe. At the last count there were 86.

When the mine finally shut in 1986 the village shook. When the new road between Gigot and Ventrèche was finished in 1991, it fell into the abyss. Leaving nothing behind but a few bitter men like Jean Marc, Francis Conda and Bernard Clé. Committed Crêpian women such as Miss Murs and Madame Coquelicot. Plus a smattering of oddballs, like Albert Gramme the maintenance man, and Raymond Clé, the sixteen-year-old grandson of Bernard.

The only exception to this decrepit bunch was Ethel Budd. A retired nurse from Newcastle, who'd moved to the village in the mid 1990s, learned the language and grown old there like everyone else.

Not that she hadn't thought of leaving. She had, many a time. Especially when the strain of the isolation and bleakness had weakened her spirit. But her unofficial role as doctor, nurse and agony aunt had kept her here. So had her legendary poker evenings. An event that had become such a feature of village life that any mention of her returning home was met with absolute horror. And normally coincided with her miraculously winning every hand. Such was the villagers fear of losing their only form of entertainment, and indeed sanity: a round of cards over a bottle of brandy, or two, was a remarkable antidote to the long dull Crêpian winters.

Ethel Budd's story was rare though. Everyone else had either left or died. Even the priest had left and now drove over once a week in his grey Renault Modus for the weekly service. As did the supermarket delivery van. Not in a Renault Modus of course, it wouldn't fit all of Jean Marc's tins of duck in for starters, but in a Mercedes van that trundled in once a week to feed the citizens of Crêpe. An occurrence which made Jean Marc often wonder whether there was the possibility of combining the two in one holy/retail round trip. Save the planet? Save your soul? But it wasn't to be. For one the supermarket van didn't operate on a Sunday, and secondly, moving Sunday Mass to Thursday, would require a miracle.

As for Jean Marc, he could never leave. He had made a bet with Francis on his wedding day that he would die in Crêpe. Francis had matched the bet, and while it was only for a Franc, it ensured, seeing as both men were as tight and as stubborn as each other, that the census figures for Crêpe (as long as they were still alive of course) would never drop below two.

So here was Jean Marc watching TV as normal a few days after the Palmer's visit when he was disturbed by a loud horn.

'That bastard postman from Ventrèche,' he swore from his armchair.

The horn went off again.

'What time do you call this? It's nearly bloody teatime! What on earth have you been doing all day – wanking! In my day I was finished by eleven.'

When the postman did come, or when he could be bothered, he made a point of letting his presence be known. A couple of loud honks on his Citroen Berlingo followed by a large exaggerated lap round the square that sprayed white gravel over the square. Then he would stop, slam the door and proceed to arrange what few bits of post there were for the dying residents of Crêpe.

'Right you cocksucker,' Jean Marc declared getting up from his armchair and charging over to the window.

He was just about to give the postie a real piece of his mind, possibly even throw a mug of cold coffee at him, when he realised it wasn't the postman at all. It was a smartly dressed man in his late 50s standing next to an English registered navy-blue Land Rover Discovery 4.

'Good afternoon,' Jean Marc cried out from his lounge window.

'*Bonjour*,' the man replied. 'OK to park here?'

'Fine,' Jean Marc answered. 'Just a minute, I'll be down.' Then charged down the stairs nearly killing himself once again on the highly polished wooden steps.

'Jean Marc Bulot, Mayor of Crêpe,' he introduced himself for the third time that week.

'*Enchanté*,' said the man shaking his hand firmly. 'Henry Clark.'

'Pleased to meet you.'

'*Mais je me demandais si vous pouviez m'aider monsieur*?'

Jean Marc's face went blank. It wasn't that he hadn't understood him. Simply that he'd never actually heard a Brit, except a passing *Bonjour* or *Au revoir,* speak French that well. True, no Frenchman would ever speak like that: it was too stuffy and formal. But technically it was perfect.

'Certainly,' Jean Marc said in English. 'How can I help you?'

'Ah, you speak English,' the man commented rather pompously. 'We both speak French here.' He pointed to a woman sitting in the passenger side wearing a large hat that looked like a pineapple sliced in half. 'We prefer to stick to that if you don't mind. Or Italian, we speak all three."

'French is fine,' confirmed Jean Marc. He was going to mention he spoke Italian as well but the man cut him off.

'So old chap. What's going on in...What did you say it was called again?'

'Crêpe,' answered the Mayor.

'Really?' replied the man. 'Must have missed the sign.'

'There isn't one. It blew down in a storm years ago. I keep telling our oaf of a maintenance man, Albert, to fix it, but nothing ever happens. Rural life you see.'

'Ah, of course, the French proletariat. The French *worker*,' he sarcastically declared. 'Well, not to bother. Probably doesn't matter, you probably don't get many visitors anyway. Pretty place though. Nice hedges. Immaculately paved square. See you've the customary Jeanne D'Arc statue in place. Personally, I think she was a bit of a charlatan.'

Jean Marc wished he'd stayed upstairs watching TV. He'd finally met the archetypal English snob Ethel Budd had warned him about.

'I'm writing a book you see,' the man droned on. 'Hidden antique shops, restaurants, cafes, markets, bookshops. Those hidden treasures no one in the outside world ever sees.'

'Except the millions of people who come to France each year searching for exactly that,' Jean Marc was about to say but the man blathered on.

'...yes, it's called Secret Gems of France...What I want to do is encapsulate...I'm already in touch with a publisher...'

Jean Marc didn't like this man one bit. He talked too much for one and Jean Marc hated talkers. People who say nothing in a lot of words. Real bores.

On the other hand, the situation was perfectly primed for one of Madame Coquelicot's ten-year-old steaks, which according to Derek and Sandra Palmer had been: Award Winning.

'It's your lucky day,' announced Jean Marc when Clark had finished, 'we have a very fine restaurant here in Crêpe - award winning was last night's verdict.'

'Darling, what's going on?' said the sliced pineapple as she ejected herself from the car. 'Did I hear award winning?'

'*Enchanté, madame*,' crooned the Mayor. 'Jean Marc Bulot, Mayor of Crêpe.' He almost bowed.

'Cynthia Clark. Pleased to meet you.'

'The delightful Mayor here was telling me about this restaurant they have tucked away here.'

'Well let's hurry it up,' Cynthia exclaimed. 'Leicester's getting hungry.'

'Leicester?' pondered Jean Marc.

At this stage most people in the civilized world would assume Leicester to be a human being. A son or perhaps a nephew in his teens or early twenties, given the couple's age. What Jean Marc didn't expect was a drooling Spaniel with a Terry Towelling coat bounding towards him from the back seat.

'*Ah, bonjour*,' he offered to the mutt.

'Lovely, isn't he?' the woman enthused.

'Yes,' the Mayor lied. It was a well-known fact in the village that Jean Marc hated dogs of all breeds, shapes and sizes.

'He's a pedigree,' she added, stroking its belly, which gave out a sickly smell: a mixture of dog food, chocolate and scented towels.

'A reservation for two then?' said Jean Marc eager to move them on as quick as possible.

'Three!' proclaimed the man holding up three fingers, which sent the dog into an insane barking fit.

'Three?'

'Be quiet Leicester,' Henry Clark yelled. The dog obeyed immediately. 'Yes. Three. He always eats with us.'

'You mean you want a place set for the dog?' asked Jean Marc incredulously.

'He's a growing boy, aren't you Leisty,' added the woman.

'I'll phone our head chef right away,' a slightly bewildered Mayor declared.

'Is this a restaurant?' Henry Clark inquired suspiciously.

'Oh yes.'

'Michelin starred I assume,' he asked picking out a gold tinted iPhone from the inside pocket of the hideous double-breasted purple sports jacket he was wearing. 'We only dine in Michelin starred establishments, or at least recommended establishments.'

'It's more of a private restaurant,' admitted Jean Marc.

'Oh,' said Cynthia. 'A private restaurant, well Henry, I think we ought to give it a try. It could be a great find for your book.'

'Naturally,' said the man looking incredibly smug as though the entire world had been carved out of the cosmic dust to pave the way for Henry Clark and his stupid book.

'We'll look forward to it,' Jean Marc grovelled. 'But just out of interest, how did you find us? Were you lost? Or did you plan to come here? Not that it matters.'

'It was funny actually,' Cynthia started. 'We were quite happy going along the main road towards Ventrèche when at the last minute the satnav redirected us here. No idea why?'

'I prefer the old-fashioned maps myself,' interrupted Clark. 'But Cynth here doesn't trust them - says they are outdated like me.'

They both laughed. Even the dog barked itself senseless again.

'Quiet Leisty,' demanded Cynthia, her thick glossy scarlet lipstick glistening in the sun. 'I think I must have flicked the satnav onto scenic mode by accident. Amazing isn't it these days. We simply turn on a machine and follow it. Takes all the hassle out of it.'

'Takes the fun out of it more like,' complained Clark in true stuffy British fashion.

'Well,' she replied. 'We wouldn't be here if it weren't for it. So count your blessings darling.'

'Agreed,' he guffawed and turned towards the Mayor, who'd become distracted by another car coming down the road.

'Can you excuse me for a minute, I think we've another visitor.'

The Mayor strode over to a rather beat up Renault Espace 3.0 dCi now parked a good distance away from the Land Rover Discovery. Clearly there was still some sort of class war raging at the heart of British society, but he could discuss that with Ethel Budd later.

'Bonsoir,' said Jean Marc greeting the driver. Another middle-aged man. This time with an uncontrollable beard and a thicket of grey hair, sweating profusely.

'Is this Ventrecht?' he said rudely wiping his saturated forehead with a filthy towel.

'No sir,' said Jean Marc. 'This is Crêpe.'

'Where?'

'Crêpe.'

'Never heard of it,' he snapped. 'We're trying to get to Ventech, or Ventricle. What's it called Dora?' he shouted at the woman sitting next to him.

'I don't know Alan,' the woman snivelled, her eyes puffed up like biscuits. Another family going through the torture of another family holiday in France.

'It's called Ventrèche,' Jean Marc corrected them.

'That's it,' he sneered. 'Satnav seems to have gone nuts.'

'Are you taking the scenic route by any chance?' asked the Mayor.

'The what?'

'The scenic route,' the Mayor replied. 'I only say that because it looks like you've picked up the old road that used to go from Gigot to Ventrèche via Crêpe and Plante. Before the new road was built. It's a very pleasant drive in fact.'

'I'm not bothered about the scenery mate,' cut in the man, 'just hungry. You got anywhere to eat in this gaff, my kids are starving?'

Jean Marc looked in the back to see three angry teenagers, sunburnt and hot. 'Alright,' one said. The other, a sarcastic, 'Bonjour.' The last, a girl with a small spear pierced through her nose, said nothing, and looked away out of the window.

'I'm just organising a restaurant for our other guests,' Jean Marc offered pointing to the Clarks still patting their stupid dog like they were poofing a pillow. 'How many are you. Table for five? Any pets?'

The man looked confused. 'No pets, just three children.'

'Great,' enthused the Mayor.

'Excuse me but what sort of restaurant is it?' demanded the woman tapping away on her phone. 'I can't find a listing for this village at all. It doesn't seem to be on the map.'

'We're very small you know,' the Mayor said quickly.

'I can see that,' the woman lashed out.

'It's a bistro,' exclaimed Jean Marc.

'Do you do burgers?' the man said,

'Of course,' beamed Jean Marc. 'Burgers are our speciality.' He was praying Madame Coquelicot had some burgers left over in her giant freezer from last year's summer fete.

'Where is it then?' demanded the man looking around aimlessly, focussing on the faded Bar La Boucle sign. 'Is that it?'

'No.' Jean Marc held his hands in the air. 'We're knocking that down soon. Regeneration project. But in the meantime, just follow that Land Rover. Our restaurant is the first house on right after you leave the village. Green door, can't miss it.'

'What's it called?' the woman demanded, tears streaming down her brittle face, as she still searched for answers on her phone.

'Err,' hesitated Jean Marc. 'Madame Coquelicot's.'

'You don't sound too sure?' The man looked like he was going to kill the hapless Mayor.

'I'm sure,' stuttered the Mayor. 'You see we've recently changed the name, part of our rebranding exercise.'

'Hmm. Madame Coquelicot's. Green Door, you say?' the man queried unconvinced. 'Sounds like a wild goose chase to me.'

And with that they drove off leaving Jean Marc sweating profusely wondering whether all of this was worth it. And perhaps next time he should stay put and watch TV.

Chapter 5 - Madame Coquelicot

One morning towards the end of the War, a wounded British soldier crawled, almost dead, into one of the gardens on Route De Ventrèche. A sixteen-year-old girl was reading a book in her room when she saw the injured man crawling towards the well to get a drink of water. At first, she thought he was German and so kept out of sight. Then she heard the words 'Help' and without even thinking to ask her parents who were working in the butcher's shop next door, she stole her father's wagon and drove the soldier to nearby Ventrèche where there was an allied field hospital.

At only five foot one, and too short to see out of the high wind screened Citroen van, she put a brick on the accelerator in order to kneel on the driver's seat and see out of the window. She made the journey in ten minutes flat but when she arrived, she couldn't remove the brick from the accelerator quickly enough and crashed into the barracks almost wiping out the entire British platoon stationed there.

The wounded soldier survived - just - and after the war he would often talk about the ordeal in the ancient Citroen van. Even joking that if he could have his time again, he would have taken his chances with the Nazis rather than go through that hellish journey.

The girl on the other hand walked away unharmed, and afterwards insisted on joining the war effort. Unfortunately, the war ended the following year so she went to Paris to study languages. Ten years later she returned to Crêpe and married Cyrille Coquelicot, who'd taken over her parents' butcher's shop. She never said anything about her life in Paris, except that, 'It had been fun.'

Seventy-four years later, that same girl, now ninety-two, was ferociously knocking on the door of the ancient Town Hall, 'Bulot!'

'*Merde*,' muttered Jean Marc looking worryingly at his watch. It had been three hours since he'd shunted the Henry Clark party off to her. From her banging it sounded like something had gone terribly wrong.

'Bulot! I know you're in there,' she hollered, banging on the thick door of the Town Hall.

'Just a minute Magalie,' he yelled down.

He was actually highly intrigued to find out what had happened with the Clark party. Unfortunately, she had showed up at the wrong moment, as normal. Right in the middle of his favourite quiz show, Top Pets, in which a mindless parade of idiots had to guess the names of the other contestants' pets from a list of prompts and photos about their life. Thierry from Macon was just about to win a Weber barbecue if he could guess the name of Janine from Montauban's Yorkshire Terrier.

It was primetime primitive TV at its very worst. Trite, puerile, and worthless. The sort of show you watched if you were in a coma being fed by a tube, barely aware of the world around you. Which was of course why the Mayor loved it, anything to take away the crushing circumstances of his dull life. In Jean Marc's book, the more trivial and docile the TV program, the better. And now Magalie had ruined it.

'Turn the TV off Bulot,' she rattled on from downstairs just as Thierry called out 'Sue' instead of 'Minnie' and won a clock radio instead.

'Idiot,' the Mayor blazed at the TV. 'It was her grandmother's nickname you clown. Didn't you see it written on her dog bowl?'

'Jean Marc Bulot!'

'I'm coming,' he blasted down.

Two minutes later he arrived in the foyer of the Town Hall to see the crumpled figure of Madame Coquelicot sitting on one of the ancient benches smoking a Gitane.

'You took your time,' she said fiercely. 'Top Pets more important than seeing the village's oldest citizen, mmm?'

'Ah. You do realise it's no smoking in here, Magalie. I have told you before.'

'Shut up,' she snapped throwing her fag onto the foyer floor and stubbing it out with her boot.

Jean Marc breathed in remembering that picking a fight with Magalie Coquelicot was as pointless as telling her to stop smoking. She had smoked all her life and at ninety-two could make it down from her house to the Town Hall quicker than anyone in the village, including Raymond Clé.

'Francis tells me your dog has died,' he said, trying to change the subject away from the nightmarish news he was sure she was going to tell him regarding the Clarks. What had happened? Had Madame Coquelicot sent him running up the road with a skewer up his ass? Or insulted his wife? Only for him to now write a terrible review, meaning no one would ever visit Crêpe again.

Madame Coquelicot looked at the Mayor, bafflement drifting over her ancient features. 'My dog?'

'The poodle?'

'Bloody hell Bulot,' she scolded him like she had done at school. 'Chibby died over seven years ago. What on earth have you been doing all this time?'

'Good question,' he mused. 'I thought I hadn't seen him around.'

'Her! She was a bitch.'

'Oh. Her, sorry.'

'Shows have much attention you pay to village affairs, Monsieur Mayor.' She took off her 1950s glasses from her rabbity face and glared at him. 'You hang around with that drunken wreck Conda too much. He doesn't even know what day of the week it is.'

'That's what I'm trying to change Magalie.'

'Well I wish you'd said that when you were young, you might have made something of yourself. You're a clever man Bulot. Or was. You speak three languages well, you're half good looking, you're not an alcoholic wreck. And yet you've spent your life doing nothing.'

'Well I was a postman.'

'Which is a tragedy. Posting letters when you could have been President. More stupid men have made it to the top. I mean look at François Hollande. Sarkozy.'

She lit another cigarette. Took a deep drag and blew the smoke out in a big grey plume that hung in the vestibule of the Town Hall like a cumulonimbus.

'So,' he breathed in anticipating the worst. 'How was the meal?'

She grinned and he felt her mood change instantly from one of bellicose witch to happy sixteen-year-old young girl.

He relaxed. Then felt annoyed because he was missing the second half of Top Pets. Damn woman, why couldn't she save whatever was so urgent until the morning. There was never anything on TV then.

'It was absolutely top notch,' she beamed. 'Magnifique! "A delightful culinary find among the crumbling ruins of a decaying French village."

'That's what the fat man with the stupid hat said. The idiot writing a book.'

'Clark,' Jean Marc smiled as he looked up towards the thick mass of dust and cobwebs gathering on the Town Hall ceiling that hadn't been cleaned in a million years.

'I don't know what he was called. But he enjoyed it so much he even left a tip.'

'A tip?' asked Jean Marc astonished. 'What do you mean a tip; you didn't charge them did you?'

'Of course, I charged them.' Madame Coquelicot's face contorted. 'After those other two gannets from the night before, I wasn't going to do it again for nothing. I'm not a charity you know.'

'How much did you charge them?'

'Thirty Euros a head, including wine. Seemed fair seeing as they were eating my prime horse meat.'

Jean Marc nearly fell over. 'Tell me you didn't feed them horse meat Magalie. Please.'

'What's the problem?'

'You know what the English are like. They won't eat anything that can run faster than them.'

'They didn't seem to mind the rate they wolfed it down.'

'Yes, but they didn't know what it was. Plus the family had a sticker on the back of their car advertising some horse sanctuary,' Jean Marc wailed.

'Mmm,' mused Madame Coquelicot. 'They did look like horses.'

'Exactly. We could be arrested for cannibalism.'

Madame Coquelicot burst out laughing. 'That's a good one Bulot. I wondered where your sense of humour had gone to.'

'I'm not joking, Magalie, this is serious. Imagine if the health inspectors came around and found out we were serving horse meat dressed up as beef.'

'Calm down Jean Marc.'

'Why couldn't you just give them beef like you gave to Derek and Sandra bloody Palmer?'

Madame Coquelicot said nothing.

'You didn't?' groaned the Mayor.

'It was the first thing I found in the freezer. It's knee-deep in meat in there. I wasn't going to start rummaging around. If I'd got stuck, I'd have frozen to death in minutes. It's the first thing I found, a nice side of horse.'

Jean Marc wondered if he should start taking those heart pills Ethel Budd had given him. Although thinking about it, they were probably almost as out of date as the contents of Madame Coquelicot's freezer.

'Magalie. Look. If we do this again, which we probably won't, please please please stick to beef. Or lamb, or pig, or chicken. Or anything that doesn't run quickly. Even if you have to freeze to death finding it. Or failing that tell me and I'll go out and kill something with my bare hands.'

'You wouldn't know how.'

'I can try,' he insisted. 'Save having a riot on our hands if those fussy Brits found out.'

'Agreed,' she said puckering her ancient lips that had the texture of barnacles. But I did make three hundred Euros.'

The Mayor's eyes bulged like billiard balls. 'Three hundred Euros,' he drooled. The horse meat incident forgotten instantly as the lethal drug of money coursed through the Mayor's shrunken veins. 'But how?'

'Four adults, three kids and a dog,' she totted up smiling.

'You charged full price for the dog?' Jean Marc exclaimed.

'Of course,' she snorted. 'And those snotty children. Plus the man with the lisp, the one writing the book, gave me a twenty Euro tip, which bumped the whole affair up to three hundred.'

'I don't think it was a lisp, I think that was what the English call posh.'

'Ah. I thought I was having trouble understanding him. And what perfume was his wife wearing? Smelt like she had doused herself in cheap brandy.'

Jean Marc laughed. 'I think that was the smell from the dog.'

'He was happy with his horse lungs anyway,' she tittered. 'Maybe that old fart might write a review in some fancy London magazine. Horse lungs en croute.'

'You're a genius Magalie,' Jean Marc sniggered again. Then inhaled deeply. 'But let's not mention the H word again. We'll end up in prison if we get caught serving horse when it's meant to be beef. I'm not the type for solitary confinement. I've had enough of that living here.'

'The only place I'm going is there.' She pointed vaguely towards the cemetery behind the church. 'If they want me, they'll have to dig me up.'

'Along with all the other crooks buried there,' he grinned. 'Incredible the priest can still call it a churchyard with all the mean hearted bastards laid in it.'

Madame Coquelicot shot him a fierce glare. 'My husband's buried in there you know.'

'So is my father and mother and I'd like to be buried there too, not cremated in some dark hellhole prison in Macon or Lisieux. So promise, no more horse talk.'

'I won't say another word,' she agreed blowing out another plume of smoke.

'Good,' he declared, although he wasn't sure he believed her. 'Right, I think it's time for a drink at Francis' house. I don't drink, but on this occasion, I'll happily raid Francis' wine cupboard.'

'How about Top Pets?' she glanced at her watch knowingly. Even the educated Madame Coquelicot couldn't resist a slice of banality served up on a silver platter.

'It can wait, Magalie. Let's get drunk instead.'

She was shocked. In all the years she had known him - which was in fact all his life - she had never known him so happy. Certainly not happy enough to make him miss his favourite TV show in favour of a drink round Francis Conda's hovel. Something was definitely afoot in the village of Crêpe.

Chapter 6 - The Crêpe Catering Committee

A week after the eventful Henry Clark visit, Jean Marc announced a meeting of the newly formed Crêpe Catering Committee. The CCC consisted of Jean Marc Bulot, director; Francis Conda, barman; Isabelle Murs, waitress; Albert Gramme, waiter; Magalie Coquelicot, chef.

They didn't know this yet. But they would in a minute.

'I summon you here today,' commenced the Mayor. 'To announce the formation of The Crêpe Catering Committee in a bid to revive our glorious village.'

Not a sound. Not even the twitch of a nose. Or a raised eyebrow. Or a murmur. He hadn't expected a round of applause, but perhaps a bit more enthusiasm.

Nevertheless, he continued. 'Due to the area's recent economic boom. The ground is fertile for local businesses to start harvesting the profits of this potential growth...'

'Well read,' interrupted Francis. 'I think I got that pamphlet through my door as well.'

'So did I,' quipped Albert Gramme. 'Last month's Gigot County Bulletin, wasn't it?'

'Month before I think,' agreed the ex-miner.

'Thank you for your contributions gentlemen,' Jean Marc reproached the two men. 'But as Madame Coquelicot will confirm, we've had a wave of visitors to the village lately and we want to make the most of it.'

'What three?'

'Ten actually, Francis,' snapped Jean Marc. 'Eleven if you include Leicester.'

'Leicester?' That confused the old drunk, who Jean Marc assumed was probably already blasted. 'Didn't they win the English football league?'

'It's a dog,' confirmed Madame Coquelicot.

'Oh I'm sorry Mags,' replied Francis sarcastically. 'That makes all the difference then. Three cars, ten humans and a dog - so we're the new Las Vegas, are we?'

'I can't believe you, Francis,' howled Jean Marc. 'Last week you thought it was a great idea. And you Magalie.' He looked at the old woman. 'Now both of you don't seem to care less.'

'Last week was last week Jean Marc,' Francis proclaimed. 'And a week is a long time in Crêpe. This hasn't been the first time you've decided to revive the village and given up after a week.'

Jean Marc stood bolt upright. 'How dare you Francis Conda. Why don't you do something for a change instead of sitting around all day drinking Pineau.'

A chorus of 'Oohs' went round the room. Then the sound of Francis' chair scraping on the parquet floor as he slowly stood up and pumped his broad frame full of air like a Michelin man getting ready to change fifty tyres at once.

'You little squirt,' he bawled. 'I've done more work than you Jean Marc Bulot in a single day than you've done in your whole lifetime. I was the first to work the mine when it opened in 1965 and the last to leave it when it closed in 1986. I drank with those Italians till five in the morning, then we would all shave, eat, have coffee and head back down the pit again for a gruelling twelve-hour shift. Then back up and straight to the bar. And all the time, what were you doing Jean Marc Bulot? Delivering love letters and postcards with fifty days off a year on a nice La Poste salary. Finish by eleven then a game of boules with your postie chums for an hour then back to the telly. Slab of steak cooked up by mummy.

'Bah. You don't even know the meaning of a full day's work. To you work is playtime in between mealtimes and bedtime. Pushing tonka toys round the living room floor or playing with your tea set. To be honest I can't even remember why we're even friends.'

'Circumstance,' Jean Marc threw back at him without a pause. 'The misfortune of being born in the same village on the same day in the same year. A village neither of us left and where all our other friends are dead. The only reason our friendship exists is that there's no one else.'

'Ooo,' echoed around the dusty chamber once again. They'd all watched this glorious soap opera between the two men numerous times, but still enjoyed it.

'Life's a bitch isn't it,' Francis countered. 'And to think of all my real friends who drank themselves to death or got chewed up in some hideous machinery down the mine. Such a waste. And all I'm left with is you. A postman.'

'It's hard for me as well Francis. Left with a drunk. Picking up all those beer bottles scattered around the village every morning.'

'Well you've got nothing else to do.'

Another round of Oohs. That was a good one they thought.

'Well Albert has. He's got hedges to trim and flower beds to weed. And he's sick of picking all your crap up every morning. Isn't that correct, Albert?'

Albert Gramme said nothing – it wasn't the time to pick sides.

'Thank you thank you gentlemen.' It was Madame Coquelicot. 'I think we've heard all of this before. Now sit down, both of you.'

The two men sat down immediately.

'So, Jean Marc, you were saying?'

When the Mayor had finished explaining his grand vision of the village with only a few more minor interruptions from Francis, which were quickly quelled by Madame Coquelicot, Albert's hand shot up as quick as a bullet fired out of a rifle.

'Yes Albert,' said the Mayor.

'I'd just like to remind you,' started Albert. 'That I'm the village maintenance man and I have a clear job description which does not, or so I'm aware, involve working in a restaurant as a waiter. I would like to say that now.'

Jean Marc sighed and folded his long thin arms against his slim chest. On the pedestal at the far end of the committee room he looked like a monkey about to perform tricks.

'All I have to do Albert is change your job description from trimming hedges to clearing tables.'

'I'll phone the union then.'

'Be my guest. The last employee who did that had to wait two years for an appointment. By which time he was dead. Your predecessor in fact, but if you insist, the union rep's number is on my notice board on a piece of faded yellow paper.'

'But why now?' pleaded Albert rather frantically. 'As Francis said, there's no one here. Three people.'

'Ten,' corrected the Mayor.

'Well, three groups totalling ten people,' clarified Albert.

'And a dog,' said Magalie.

'That's beside the point,' continued the Mayor, 'ten today. Fifty tomorrow. Next year, a thousand. You only need a few good reviews on Tourist Trader and you're in.

'What's Tourist Trader?' questioned the maintenance man.

'It's one of those review sites where people get a chance to complain about dirty forks or the mayonnaise sachets being the wrong brand. Ventrèche has four out of five stars, believe it or not.'

'So, this is all about beating Ventrèche, is it?' asked Francis inquisitively.

'Not at all,' defended the Mayor. 'This is all about resurrecting this mighty village to its glory days.'

'When were they?' asked Miss Murs.

'Don't you remember, Miss Murs?'

'I was three in 1970 Jean Marc and according to my mother these so-called glory days consisted of a load of Italians getting drunk on Pineau and feeling up girls. Those glory days you mean?'

'Yes, those glory days,' Jean Marc declared defiantly. 'At least there were some girls to feel up Miss Murs.'

Miss Murs glared back. At fifty-two, she had luckily escaped the antics of the Italian miners. Although saying that she probably wouldn't have minded it. Simply because by the time she was ready to marry, everybody had gone.

Francis stood up again. 'Look. The only reason Crêpe even had a heyday or glory days as you put it, is because that fat git Maurice Lafarge found a seam of coal the width of a slice of flan on his land while digging for potatoes. If he'd been digging for parsnips in his other field, he would have never found it, would never have sold it to the coal board, never become rich, never become mayor, and Crêpe would have slipped into the Dark Ages years ago.'

'What are you saying?' flapped Jean Marc. 'We were lucky?

'That's exactly what I'm saying Jean Marc. Moreover, good luck doesn't strike twice. Not for a Frenchman anyway. So you'd better get used to it. Because this is all we've got.' Francis let out a beery burpy laugh that wafted over towards the Mayor.

'You make it sound so black and white, Francis. Places always get more than one chance. It's called a renaissance. Otherwise half the country would have slipped into ruins by now.'

Francis' eyebrows shot up. 'Hasn't it already?'

Jean Marc accepted the point and sat down again. He wasn't going to argue with the grizzled ex-miner over the nation's industrial decline. There would be a fight and he would lose.

'So,' he said, the room suddenly calm after the mudslinging of the past few minutes. 'Any more questions?'

Miss Murs' hand shot up. 'Where is this restaurant going to be?'

'Here,' stated the Mayor confidently.

'What!' she wailed, 'do you know this is an official room - you can't just use it as a restaurant? It's owned by La Republique.'

Jean Marc smashed his hand down on the table much harder than he intended. 'But it's hardly ever used, Miss Murs.'

'Nor are you,' she balked raising a spate of further giggling from the others.

'Miss Murs. I hope that remark is off the record?'

'I'm not keeping any records, you told me not to. But I can note it if you want.'

'Not on this occasion thank you Miss Murs,' ordered Jean Marc quickly. 'I would prefer this meeting to be off the record.'

‘Good,’ came Albert again. ‘Because on the record or off the record I’m not doing it. I’m the maintenance man not a waiter. And neither is Miss Murs, she’s the village secretary. And Francis is the village drunk. And Madame Coquelicot is, well, just there. We’re not waiters or chefs. We’re people. You will just have to find someone else.’

‘Fine,’ said the Mayor bluntly. ‘I’ll advertise in the Gigot Post tomorrow. One barman, two waiters, one chef. I’m sure there are lots of people looking for a job.’

‘But Jean Marc,’ whined Albert. ‘Why all the rush.’

‘Don’t you want to do something with your life?’ exploded Jean Marc standing up again. ‘Something more than being a maintenance man. Or a village secretary. Or a drunk.'

Miss Murs stood up. ‘I was all set to go to Paris remember to become a translator like Madame Coquelicot. Or even a dancer. Weren't you a dancer, Magalie? You were, weren't you? I know it.'

Madame Coquelicot stared straight ahead.

'I wanted to be something. Somebody. Except on the morning my train left for Paris my parents fell mysteriously ill and I never left Crêpe. You all know the story anyway. I don't even know why I'm bothering to tell it again.'

‘We all remember, Isabelle,’ Jean Marc concluded mournfully. ‘And a tragic waste. But at least you’re here now, Miss Murs, and for that we are all grateful.’

Albert however, wasn’t so grateful. ‘Please yourselves. Find someone else from Gigot or Ventrèche if you must. I’m quite happy with what I’ve got.’

Jean Marc started packing up his file containing a single piece of paper. ‘Fine. I just thought you all might want to earn a few extra Euros that’s all. But I’m quite happy running it myself and taking all the profits.

The room fell silent.

'Remind us Madame Coquelicot,' said the Mayor quietly. 'How much we made on that first night? Bearing in mind there were only seven people and a dog in attendance.'

'Three hundred Euros,' she said emphatically.

'Why didn't you say that in the first place?' Francis exploded. 'Why didn't you say, "Here's a sure-fire way to make a huge wad of cash," instead of all this Make Crêpe Better Crap?'

'Yeh,' said Albert. 'If I had known that.'

'I thought it was obvious,' bellowed Jean Marc. 'We open a restaurant and earn money. It's kind of basic, isn't it?'

The room went quiet again as they chewed over the implications. All five present had all worked for the state. Jean Marc for La Poste and now the Town Hall along with Albert Gramme and Miss Murs. Madame Coquelicot had worked for the education board. And Francis Conda the coal board. Meaning no one had ever really considered they could actually work for themselves.

'You mean, we could keep the money we make?' summed up Albert. 'And the more we make the more we can keep.'

'Yes. It's called free enterprise,' declared the Mayor.

'When can we start?' asked Albert now as keen as freshly spread Dijon mustard.

'Well. Tonight,' declared Jean Marc.

The room darkened. The sky blackened. Imaginary chains swayed from hooks. The curtains ruffled. The atmosphere became as thick as jam as the spectre of a full day's work stalked the premises.

'I'm sorry,' fumbled Albert. 'You mean now, as in...'

'...as in today Albert. As in right now.'

'But...' Albert was stumped for words.

'Yes, I know it's amazing, but there is such a word as spontaneity.'

‘But we can’t just start now,’ stuttered the maintenance man.

‘He's right,' added Miss Murs. 'How about work contracts and health assessments. You can’t just start a business up in a day. How about all the rules and regulations? And tax?'

'Haven't you been listening to a word I've been saying? Free enterprise. We keep what we make. And shove two fingers up at the taxman.'

'But isn't that illegal?' questioned the secretary.

Jean Marc's eyebrows shot up. 'Not if he doesn't know Miss Murs. That’s why I insisted you don’t take any notes. Don’t you see. This is going to be our business. You know, OUR business,’ he repeated.

‘Ahh,’ came from the floor. The realisation of what Jean Marc was saying finally dawned on them. It had taken nearly three hours, but they had finally got there.

'What shall we call it?' bleated Albert smiling.

Jean Marc shrugged. 'I don't know, I haven't gotten that far yet. How about Le Restaurant?'

Chapter 7 - Le Restaurant

'I'm off,' declared Francis from behind the makeshift bar they'd fashioned from an old upright piano and a couple of floorboards.

'Me too,' agreed Albert dressed in a white shirt, black trousers and a pink plastic carnation he'd found in the Town Hall lost property box. A wooden champagne crate that over thirty years had managed to amass half a dozen items: A few broken pencils, a 1995 motoring Atlas, the head of a plastic doll, a day pass for the Trocadero (lapsed), a set of car keys and a bunch of plastic flowers. 'Such a stupid idea.'

'Agreed,' creaked Miss Murs looking down at her pitchfork black full-length dress that had belonged to her mother. 'Feels like I'm waiting on my own funeral.'

'It suits you,' commented Madame Coquelicot from behind her large metal skillet and a two-ring hob they'd put on top of the Mayor's pedestal at the back of the committee room. 'It makes you look slim, Isabelle.'

'I am slim,' countered Miss Murs glaring at the old woman who despite standing behind a fifteen-inch skillet was dressed immaculately as always. On this occasion wearing an emerald and mauve two-piece tweed suit complete with feathered hat and a selection of pearls and necklaces.

‘I’d just prefer to be wearing something less constricting,’ continued the secretary. ‘Like nothing. I’m normally in bed by now.’

‘Well you won’t have to wait much longer,’ the Mayor forecasted looking at his watch. Then glumly down at his own attire: A 1967 Pierre Cardin suit he had worn for his own wedding and which he’d bought on his only trip to Paris. Which incredibly still fitted and was another benefit of Crêpe's isolation from the modern world. Not only did dogs not dine with their owners here, but also, the lack of shops, bakeries or butchers, plus a once a week delivery van, meant no one really bothered eating unless it was absolutely necessary.

‘Eight forty-five and not a soul,’ he groaned taking the red plastic rose out of his lapel and tossing it on the bar top next to Francis’ row of freshly polished wine glasses. ‘May as well have worn a pink monkey suit.’

‘Drink?’ offered Francis lifting a large bottle of Cote du Rhone off the counter and pouring the Mayor and himself an extremely large glass.

His best friend was right. Maybe he should drink himself to death. There was little else to live for. His big idea had fallen flat on its face like a man falling from a thirty-story building with a piano attached to his neck.

'Anyone else?' asked Francis.

'Why not,' said Albert, who also rarely drank. 'I feel pretty down to be honest. I know I complained at first but I’ve never been a waiter before and once we got all set up, I was looking forward to it.’

‘I felt the same,’ admitted the drunk who was also looking very smart, dressed in a tuxedo he’d found in his loft. ‘When we got towards opening time, I felt a tingle of nerves that actors probably get on the first night. Then when the curtain went up and there was no one there, I felt a huge sadness well up in me. As though my audience had let me down.'

'Ufff. Well sorry for ruining the party,' laughed Miss Murs pouring herself a glass. 'But I'm pretty over the moon about it to be honest. I wasn't looking forward to it in the slightest. Glad it's all over.'

'Bully for you Isabelle,' crowed Madame Coquelicot from behind her pedestal. 'But I agree with the boys, it could have been a hoot. Not much else happens round here does it?'

'I would rather have been in bed.'

'You've been in bed all your life girl,' boomed the old school mistress who had taught everyone in the room. 'It's time to wake up Isabelle Murs - smell the coffee.'

'I actually prefer tea, Madame,' Miss Murs mocked her old teacher. 'But only in the morning. So I think I'll leave you to it. And you can take that stupid bunting down from the ceiling.' She pointed to the Tricolore and Union Jack bunting they'd hung up from the oak beams that afternoon. Decorations left over from the VE day celebrations over twenty years ago.

'It looks pathetic, like ancient fishing lines in the rotting hull of a trawler. Remember this is meant to be a committee room not some tawdry Texas steakhouse. It's state territory by the way, I checked it. If the President ever paid us a visit, we could be done for treason.'

'Miss Murs,' snapped the Mayor. 'Don't be absurd. It's not state property, it's the property of Crêpe for use by the residents of Crêpe to make their impoverished lives less painful.'

The Mayor checked his watch again and took a gigantic swig of wine. 'I think we're done,' he concluded. 'You can all go home.'

He too was feeling flat. As flat as the candles he'd lit on the seven tables hours ago and which now resembled squashed field mushrooms they had burnt down so low.

'I should have got on that train,' Miss Murs mumbled to herself putting on her coat over her dress. 'The day I stayed here was the worst decision of my life. I should have just got on that train and gone to Paris and to hell with looking after my stupid and now dead parents. What a waste of a life. And you're right Madame Coquelicot, I am still slim and still have breasts. Maybe I'll still go to Paris and marry someone rich!' She was staring directly at the Mayor for some reason.

But he wasn't listening any more. He was looking at the row of empty wine glasses glistening in the dying flames of the candles.

'Francis,' he said slowly. 'Do you see anything?'

'Yes, an empty restaurant.'

'No,' scowled the Mayor looking at the glasses. 'They're vibrating. Look!'

Francis looked at the row of glasses. His eyes weren't what they used to be, but he could see them moving alright. 'Heavens above, you're right,' he agreed. 'What do you think it is? Maybe an earthquake or some mine subsidence. I was only speaking to Bernard the other day and he swore he could feel movement below the surface....'

'Shut up a minute,' the Mayor blazed. 'Listen.' Jean Marc was now whispering. 'Can you hear something?

'You're right.' It was Miss Murs. Now recovered from her stroppy teenage fit.

'I think you're all hearing things,' rattled Madame Coquelicot, who was now frying herself the biggest steak out of the lot.

'No, he's right,' agreed Albert signalling everybody to be quiet. 'Sshh.'

Jean Marc wasn't sure why everyone was being so quiet; they were running a restaurant not a cemetery. But the situation had become so terribly tense they were all scared witless of making a wrong move at the wrong moment.

'Go to the door,' Francis advised.

The Mayor rushed to the door, wine glass in hand, put his ear to it and listened hard. He had an old record player which he listened to his old Jacques Brel records on. When the record had finished and the dead Belgian singer had signed off for the night, the whole unit hummed for ten minutes like an old fridge until it went dead.

This was a similar sound. Except stronger, deeper, and it was getting louder by the minute.

'Stay where you are,' he ordered and rushed outside into the square and when he saw them, he sank to his knees shattering his kneecaps on the limestone slabs. But he didn't care. He could have been skewered, salted and barbecued, and he wouldn't have felt anything. Up ahead he saw the glare of a thousand headlights.

'Hallelujah,' he cried out as a convoy of campers, cars, caravans, and ice-cream-white motor homes chugged down the road towards Crêpe like the tanks did in 1940.

'Action stations,' cried Jean Marc as he ran back inside. 'To the ready; there's an army approaching.'

'Bugger,' Miss Murs swore, tightening up her pinafore and reinserting her carnation back into her dead mother's black funeral dress. 'And why are you hobbling? You're bleeding at the knees,' she asked the Mayor.

'Don't worry about me Miss Murs. Just get ready. And Madame Coquelicot, put that steak back - they're for customers. Albert. Francis. Ready?'

'Yes, sir,' they cried out in unison with no sarcasm in their voices whatsoever. In fact, for the first time in their lives they both sounded genuinely excited.

Chapter 8 - Brits

It took five minutes for the seven tables in the committee room to be taken with a wide cross section of British society ranging from builders to retired civil servants. One particularly pompous man in the Henry Clark mould couldn't help going on about how much he enjoyed, 'Roughing it with the plebs.'

In other circumstances it might have caused a riot. But everyone was in such good spirits that even the hardest men seemed to laugh it off as just a bit of light hearted banter between compatriots. Their good nature heightened of course by Madame Coquelicot's seventy-year-old-cast-iron-skillet-cooked steaks and Francis Conda's extra-large glasses of wine.

It was incredible. Within half an hour of everyone arriving it felt like the restaurant had been around for decades. A well-established family bistro with Albert rushing from table to table like a seasoned Parisian waiter. Francis uncorking bottles and pouring wine like an experienced sommelier. Even Miss Murs in her dead mother's dress and a pained expression splashed all over her face like a bad watercolour seemed to be enjoying it.

The only problem was a lack of tables. After the fold-up tables they'd carted up from the basement and set up in the Town Hall's foyer had been occupied, people started to sit outside in the square. As nine o'clock moved onto ten, the cars and vans and campers kept on coming, it wasn't long before the normally deserted *Place de Crêpe* resembled a festival site. The once pristine limestone slabs were now streaked with red wine and steak blood as though everybody had been mown down by a firing squad.

At eleven o'clock Jean Marc decided to close. Not because they wanted to - on the contrary, Jean Marc had been waiting for something like this for ten years - but simply because they'd run out of everything. Every hamburger, steak and sausage and every ancient box of Cote du Rhone and out-of-date Kronenbourg they'd dragged up from the cellar, had been eaten or drunk.

'Albert,' Jean Marc cried out to the sweating waiter. 'Ring the bell and tell everyone we're closing in twenty minutes.'

'What bell?' asked Albert, carrying a stack of plates as high as the Eiffel Tower.

'The bell above the Town Hall.'

'Jean Marc, there is no bell. There hasn't been a bell there since the war.'

'Really? OK, ring the church bells then. The control box is in my office. Don't bother with the settings just press the big red button that says RING.'

Despite Crêpe's penchant for loitering in the Dark Ages, the church had one of the most advanced electronic bell ringing systems in the region. A present courtesy of the Catholic Church to ensure even dead-end places like Crêpe got out of bed in the morning. Not that anyone did, of course.

'But won't it wake the villagers?' considered Albert. 'It's late.'

Jean Marc laughed. 'Don't be ridiculous Albert. No one's been awake here since 1989.'

Albert accepted the point and headed into Jean Marc's dusty rabbit warren of an office to activate the four ancient bells. Or two of them anyway. The other two had dead birds or slate wedged in giving out a couple of dull thuds rather than sonorous bassy chimes.

Within seconds Francis' makeshift bar was besieged, leaving Jean Marc staring in astonishment. So, this was the famous Last Orders Ethel Budd had told him about: The absurd ritual where at the stroke of eleven o'clock everybody rushes to the bar to order three pints each just in case the planet was about to explode and deny them their last chance to get really drunk.

'But I've run out of booze,' Francis cried to Jean Marc as a gaggle of hot faced Englishmen and women thrust their glasses in his face.

'What have you got at home?' demanded Jean Marc.

Francis looked like a ghost had run through him. 'Not my private collection!'

'We've no choice. Just get it please.'

'Why?' Francis implored.

'Because if we don't, we'll have a riot on our hands. Now for once, Francis Conda, please do as I say.'

Chapter 9 - Cash

‘Wow,’ said Jean Marc sitting down after everybody had gone. 'What an evening.'

'What fun,' cried Madame Coquelicot, her entire outfit covered in grease and beef fat. ‘Such nice people as well.'

'Drunks more like,' added Francis, distraught his once fine array of wines had been reduced to the single bottle he’d hidden below the bar before the stampede.

‘It’s increased our profits by 10%,’ Jean Marc remarked. ‘If this last orders business happens every night we’ll be rich. Thank God for the British. If they had been French, we'd be still faffing around with coffee and small portions of tart au citron.'

'I'm sorry?' questioned Francis pouring a large glass of wine from his remaining bottle. 'What do you mean: "If this happens every night."' He mimicked his friend's jaunty accent.

Jean Marc looked genuinely confused. 'What else do you think I’m talking about? We do plan to open every night Francis.'

Francis raised his head and shot his friend such an evil look it could have nailed him to the cross hanging on the wall behind him. Then let out a loud shriek of laughter that split Madame Coquelicot eardrums in half as she'd just turned her hearing aids up to full after switching them off during the service. 'Ha ha ha. It's a joke, isn't it? Good one. You almost got me there.'

'No joke.'

Francis stopped laughing.

'Running a restaurant Francis is not just a one-day event like a Tombola at a village fete.'

'I thought it was just a one-off. An occasional thing.'

'What happens on all the other days?' challenged the Mayor.

'We send them to Ventrèche like we always do.'

'That's precisely why we'll open every day, seven days a week if we have to. We can crush Ventrèche once and for all.'

'I see,' murmured Francis pouring another glass of wine, 'So this whole escapade is really to get one over Ventrèche and nothing to do with reviving Crêpe.'

'It's both if you must know. And why not, what's Ventrèche ever done for us, Francis?'

'I have friends in Ventrèche. Good friends.'

'So do I,' the Mayor lied.

'No you don't.'

'Yes, I do. Violette lives there.'

'Hardly a friend,' muttered Miss Murs. 'Leaving you like that. Running off to Ventrèche with that toad Michel Arnold.'

'I think that's my business Miss Murs,' he said sternly. 'And anyway Francis, I thought you liked it. What happened to being at the theatre?'

'But I don't fancy doing it every night. I'm sure actors are absolutely sick of it by the final curtain.'

'Fine,' confirmed the Mayor. 'One barman required. I'll put an ad in the Gigot Post first thing tomorrow. Anyone else. Madame Coquelicot? Miss Murs? Albert?'

'Oh no, I'm in,' enthused Madame Coquelicot.

'Albert?'

'Do I have a choice?'

'Not really. Miss Murs?'

Francis was banking on Miss Murs saying no so as to make it a fifty-fifty split against the Mayor. Not that he wanted to make life difficult for his lifelong friend. He loved him really. But the truth was, he simply couldn't help going against him at any given opportunity. A built-in contrariness learnt in the cold playground when they were growing up. Jean Marc would make a suggestion of a game of hopscotch only for Francis to insist on conkers.

'Miss Murs?' pressed Jean Marc.

'I have to agree with Albert. I was nonplussed at the start as I said but I have to say I did enjoy it. It was quite fun - yes, it was like Paris might have been.'

'But every day Miss Murs,' Francis pleaded. 'Every day of the week.' He said it like it was a death sentence.

'We get paid for it, don't we?' she exclaimed looking at Jean Marc expectantly.

'Ah hang on a minute,' said Francis standing up quickly. 'I know your game Jean Marc Bulot. Come on, hand it over."

'It's in the Town Hall safe,' said the Mayor too quickly.

'There isn't a safe,' boomed Francis. 'Everyone knows that. It's in your pocket. Hand it over. If I'm going to do this - and I haven't agreed yet - I want paying and I want my wine cellar restocked before I do anything. And from now on all profits are split equally. Let's have a vote on it. All for yes, raise your hand.'

'Just a minute,' complained Jean Marc. 'I'm the Mayor, I make these types of decisions.'

'As a citizen of Crêpe,' rallied Francis. 'I'm making an executive order. Who votes for all profits to be split equally? Hands in the air.'

'There's no such thing as an executive order,' complained the Mayor.

All four hands went up.

'Bastards,' he muttered, his hope of a five-star trip to Hawaii, a dream since he'd seen a poster in a travel agent in Gigot with his parents when he was sixteen, destroyed by his so-called friends. Those needle thin palm trees reaching for the sky, the beautiful brown-haired girls in their tight bikinis, the screenwash-coloured sea. All slipping away into the brown, sodden clays of Crêpe.

'That's settled then. Get the loot out,' demanded Francis.

Jean Marc sagged forward further like a small bone had been removed from his neck. 'Bloody theft this is, it was my idea in the first place, no one else thought of it,' he ranted on as he dug out a wad of notes and loose change from his pocket. 'If it hadn't been for me, you would be all sitting in front of the TV eating your tinned Potato Dauphinois.'

'And the other pocket!' ordered Francis. 'I know how many people we had here, and at twenty-five Euros a head, I reckon we took over fifteen hundred.'

He wasn't far off. 1596 Euros in actual fact, including tips and money dropped on the floor while people drunkenly fumbled for change.

'And I suggest Miss Murs manages the money from now on and divides it equally at the end of the night,' Francis angled his gaze towards Jean Marc.

'I'm capable of doing that,' Jean Marc declared looking at the stash of cash on the table.

'I think not,' Francis insisted. 'Miss Murs has managed the Town Hall accounts for years, she's the only person for the job.'

'That's fine,' the Mayor said. 'Let her put it all through the books in her lovely swirly handwriting, that way the local director of public finance will be perfectly able to read how much tax we owe him. Didn't you people understand a word of what I was saying this morning? This is OUR business.'

'But what happens if I get caught?' she questioned, looking frightened.

'Look, if anybody asks,' advised Jean Marc. 'Tell them the restaurant is a community project to raise money for homeless children in Burkina Faso. If that doesn't work, say the church organized it. Let them deal with it.'

'Just one thing though.'

'Yes Albert.'

'Will we have a day off?'

'Yes,' said Jean Marc quickly and then paused to add some gravitas to the next line. 'In October.'

'In October!' the four cried out.

'But you'll have the whole winter off.'

Francis was going to mention that he had the whole winter off anyway. And the summer. But he stopped himself. Perhaps for once, and possibly for the first time in his life, Jean Marc had got this one right.

'Just one more thing?'

'Yes, Albert. And please make it the last thing. I think we are all very tired now.'

'Will Miss Murs and I get the whole winter off as well?

'Well of course not, you're contracted to the Marie of Crêpe. But I wouldn't worry about it,' Jean Marc concluded smiling, his two gold molars gleaming in the overly bright lights of the restaurant/committee room.

'It's not that you have a lot to do anyway. And plus by the winter time we might all be so rich we might be able to move to somewhere nice. Or simply hang up our boots and kick back until next year.'

'Next year!'

Chapter 10 - Le Overflow

A week later, Jean Marc and Miss Murs broke into the old guesthouse. Or more accurately smashed the door down with a sledgehammer they'd found in the cellar. The keys having long since vanished along with any evidence as to who actually owned the building.

During the war - as Sandra Cassidy had correctly pointed out - it had served as a Gestapo prison. The local commander having lived one hundred metres away in the apartment above the Town Hall. After a morning of interrogation and torture he regularly lunched in a restaurant on the *Place de Crêpe* which later became Bar La Boucle.

After the war the building fell into ruin. Until, in the mid 1950s, an intensely Catholic family from Paris, keen to make a go of country life for their three young boys, bought it and moved in.

They didn't last long. Mainly because they had assumed rural France was as Catholic as they were. Crêpe a hotbed of hard work, religious zeal and abstinence. They were wrong. Crêpe was just another sleazy French village, ladened with laziness, meanness, madness and alcoholism. Most people only went to mass because it was something to do. And a perfect excuse to go to the bar afterwards.

Their excessive politeness and eagerness to help out with absolutely everything from harvesting to teaching, preaching to ploughing, soon made them intensely hated. And when their sons started school and got half beaten to death by the 'rough country' boys, they soon fled back to the safety of Neuilly-sur-Seine.

The house remained empty for another ten years before the mining company bought it and converted it into a boarding house for the Abruzzi miners. After the colliery closed in 1986, it was sold back to the village for a song. Then flogged off to a Swedish bachelor by Monsieur Lafarge and six months later sold on to an English family for three times the amount the bachelor had bought it for. Prompting most to assume the Swedish bachelor and Monsieur Lafarge were in fact the same person. It was never proved but when the old Mayor died and Jean Marc took over his office, a certain Eric Egrafal kept cropping up in various accounts and documents. Naively assuming it to be the Swedish gentlemen and that Lafarge had done nothing wrong, Jean Marc thought nothing of it. Until one day he saw a document in the office mirror. Egrafal was not some ancient Swedish surname at all, it was Lafarge spelt backwards. Eric, a half-arsed anagram of Maurice. How utterly stupid of him. So utterly predictable, and yet no-one, not even Jean Marc, a self-confessed addict of turgid police dramas, had seen Lafarge's feeble ruse.

After digging deeper to try and find where the money had gone, he discovered a second Town Hall account which had been emptied on the day he died by his wife, who went to live in Gigot with her sister. Jean Marc was determined to recover the money, but when she died a few months later her lawyer secretly advised Jean Marc to leave it. There was nothing left anyway. Much to the crushing disappointment of her two wayward sons, who, as Jean Marc remembered, had been the main offenders during the beatings of the poor Parisian boys.

The *Auberge de Crêpe* therefore stood empty. And even if there was no real legal paperwork or documentation to prove it, the old building had most likely been absorbed back into the village estate by default.

'But we can't use this as a restaurant Jean Marc,' declared Miss Murs.

'Why not?'

'Because it smells of shit.'

Miss Murs had total respect for the French language and would never use a word out of place or substitute another word because she couldn't be bothered to think of a suitable replacement. But in this case the word 'shit' summed up the smell of the guesthouse perfectly.

'I agree,' concurred the Mayor as he spied the rotting carcass of a cat. 'But what are we going to do? We need an overflow. The Town Hall restaurant can't cope.'

'We could use your office.'

'Too small.'

'How about your flat?'

'Too many stairs. Carting the food up and down would be impractical and downright dangerous. We need somewhere clean, nearby and preferably on the same level.'

'We could use my house.'

Jean Marc's face cracked open like an egg, a deep line appeared from his forehead to his neck and from the dark gloomy crack down the middle of his face a white dove flew out, glided past Miss Murs' ear and out into the fresh air through a broken window. 'What a brilliant idea, Isabelle.'

Miss Murs blushed. She couldn't remember the last time he'd called her Isabelle. If ever.

'It's a great idea Miss Murs,' he corrected himself. 'And right next door to the Town Hall as well. Plus, if I remember correctly your lounge shares the same wall as the conference room. I remember listening to your parents screaming at you: "Bring this, bring that!" Always followed by lots of banging.'

'That was probably me trying to climb the wall,' she laughed.

'We could knock the wall through even. Make more space.'

'Why not?' she agreed. 'I've always felt cramped in there.'

'Great! Let's go and have a look.'

The downstairs of Miss Murs house was bigger than it looked and with a few alterations like removing the sofa, armchair, bookshelves, television, and cabinets. Plus, all the other debris and junk scattered about the room, it could be fashioned into a nice dining area.

'Yes, this is perfect,' observed the Mayor looking at some pictures of mountains screwed onto the wall. 'Could even have an alpine theme.'

'My father liked the mountains,' Miss Murs explained. 'He never went of course - never went anywhere - but he liked looking at them.'

'Miss Murs?' Jean Marc asked. Then stopped himself. He couldn't believe what he was thinking. Standing there looking at the pictures he had the absurd impulse to ask her to marry him. He had never felt even an inkling of desire towards her, but as he looked back at her an image of what was behind those thick wool skirts, starched blouses and dark brooding makeup flashed before his eyes.

'I've just had this thought,' he stammered trying to regain his composure. 'That perhaps it would make sense for you to run this part of your restaurant on your own. You speak English and German so it would make sense to have this as your own setup. Let's call it a subsidiary of Le Restaurant next door. Obviously it's still part of the CCC with me as overseer of course. But this could work.'

‘I always wanted to have dinner parties but my parents wouldn't allow them.’

‘Well Miss Murs, from now on, you can have dinner parties every night.’

Miss Murs let out a giddy laugh. ‘I'll start preparing now. What time do we open?'

'Six. Be ready for six, I’m changing the opening time from seven to six. In the meantime, make sure everything's shipshape and ready to go. Think like we’re opening the Ritz.’

'But Jean Marc,' she asked looking slightly panicked as he was halfway out of the door. 'What about my secretary job and the notices?’

Jean Marc paused to think about it.

'Don’t worry about them Isabelle. No one reads them anyway.'

‘I thought so.’

Chapter 11 - La Crêperie

At six o'clock that evening Jean Marc Bulot, dressed in his freshly pressed Pierre Cardin suit, stood outside the Town Hall. Everything was set for the grand opening of *Le Overflow*. Miss Murs had tidied up the lounge and thrown away all her rubbish. Francis was dressed in a sparkling white tuxedo newly donated by Ethel Budd's nephew, Gary. Madame Coquelicot, wearing a maroon crushed velvet cocktail dress she'd bought in 1952, was busy salting and airing her steaks as she did every afternoon before service. The only person missing was Albert Gramme.

The Mayor sighed and looked up at the church bells. All he could hear was the quiet rumble of thunder over Gigot. Another hot day meant another heavy downpour later. Monstrous for the guests sloshing back and forth from their campers, but at least it saved him the job of hosing down the village square after they'd all gone to bed.

He looked up at the church tower again. Then at the digital Casio watch Francis had bought him for his fortieth birthday, which remarkably still worked, then back at the church tower. 'I should have fired that idiot years ago,' he mumbled to himself. 'Where the hell is he?'

Twenty minutes later as the clouds gathered over Crêpe and a few spots of rain started falling, the lolloping figure of

Albert Gramme came trudging up *Rue de Plante* from his house on the outskirts of the village.

'Reporting for duty, sir,' he blurted out sarcastically once he'd crossed the square and ambled up to the Mayor, thrusting his hand up to his forehead in mock salute and standing to attention.

'What time do you call this?' scolded Jean Marc trying to ignore the maintenance man's bizarre behaviour.

'Six twenty, sir,' screeched Albert.

'Let's drop the sergeant-major shit corporal,' ordered the Mayor acidly.

'Yes sir.' Albert dropped the salute and adopted his normal ungainly demeanour, his crinkle-cut, long black hair covering either side of his face like a pair of thick curtains.

'Why aren't those bells ringing?' Jean Marc demanded pointing to the church tower.

Albert looked at his watch again - which also happened to be a Casio of a very similar model. 'Because it's only six twenty,' he declared. 'The bells don't ring till seven. Is your Casio on the blink or something?'

The Mayor looked at his watch out of sheer habit, then shook his wrist out of pure annoyance. 'Albert!' he yelled, his good mood deflated by this moronic imbecile standing in front of him. 'I know what time the bells ring out. I've listened to them ring out every morning, noon and night for the past sixty-seven years.'

'So why are you asking me then?'

'Because today those bells were meant to be ringing out at six to coincide with the new restaurant opening time. Weren't you listening to a word I said this afternoon?'

The maintenance man was looking at the Mayor of Crêpe impishly. He knew exactly what the Mayor had said to him; he'd simply chosen to ignore him. As Francis had discovered years ago, the look on the Mayor's face whenever he was goaded, provoked or teased was always worth it. That same wilting expression: the sagging eyes, the wrinkled-up chin, the quivering lips. At any moment you expected his face to collapse unashamedly into a full-blown sob.

'Don't you remember anything?' the Mayor carried on waving his hands about as though he was about to produce a rabbit from a hat. 'It was meant to be my great promotional gimmick.'

'Does the priest know about this gimmick?' retorted Albert bringing his hands gently together in prayer.

'He doesn't need to know; he's never here except on Sunday mornings. Plus he doesn't even live in Crêpe. He lives in Ventrèche with all the rest. To hell with him.'

'I'm sorry,' apologised Albert walking towards the door while smirking at Francis who he could see through the window of the committee room necking a carafe of *Cote-du-Rhone* while Jean Marc was out of the room. 'You'd better do it yourself. I don't fancy experiencing the wrath of the Catholic Church. Not after what they did to Jeanne d'Arc.' He eyeballed the statue of the dead saint in the square.

'Burning you at the stake Albert would certainly bring the punters in, especially when your hair catches fire.'

'I'm not cutting my hair.'

'I'm not asking you to. I'm just asking you to do a job. But don't worry about it Albert, I'll do it. After all it's just another job to add to my list, like hosing down all the rancid steak grease, vomit and wine stains off the village square every morning while you're lying in bed.'

'Oh don't worry about that, it's starting to rain, that always does the trick.' Albert winked at the dark clouds.

'Thanks for the weather forecast,' said the Mayor bitterly. 'Just be here at six in the future.'

'But why? No one ever arrives till about six thirty. Or whatever time this glitch switches itself on.'

'*Le Glitch,*' corrected Jean Marc. 'I've called it *Le Glitch.*' The Mayor perked up. 'It's quite catchy, isn't it?'

'Oh sorry, *Le Glitch,*' Albert mimicked Jean Marc's throaty Gigot County accent that sounded like the speaker had swallowed a fish hook. 'Is *Le Glitch* another sales gimmick?'

'As a matter of fact, yes it is,' replied the Mayor confidently. 'The Gigot County Bulletin recommends drawing up seven things you can do each week to drum up business. Loyalty schemes, theme nights, minor celebrity appearances, charity events, special offers, live music are all mentioned. Even magic acts. It's vital we get away from this idle and lazy French way of thinking. We need to think more Anglo-Saxon, more dynamic, more flexible, more positive.'

'Is that why we haven't got a union?'

Jean Marc nearly slammed the solid oak Town Hall door, that weighed over two tonnes, in Albert's face. 'We don't need a union because we are the union and we work together to decide what's best for us. The last thing in the world we need is some greasy union man putting his hand into the pot, taking his subscription then telling us we have to go on strike.'

'You've become quite a ruthless businessman, haven't you? Next up you'll be selling off the Town Hall and Church to Taco Bell.

Jean Marc's eyes bulged. 'What a great idea,' he grinned. 'Which reminds me, Albert. Could you sort those bells out? Remove those birds or whatever is wedged in them. They sound awfully sinister. '

'I like them,' replied Albert defiantly. 'Sounds like the intro to Hell's Bells by AC/DC.'

Jean Marc smiled. He had heard of AC/DC - Francis liked them. He didn't. 'I would prefer them to sound more like Jingle Bells. Let's add some sparkle and magic to the place. More like Disneyland.'

'Shall I dress up as Mickey Mouse as well?'

'I think we're all dressed up enough as it is.' Jean Marc looked down at his suit. 'Even Miss Murs has made an effort tonight, dressed, I noticed, in a rather fetching red dress, red high-heels and red shawl. In fact, if this wasn't Crêpe, we might all be going to the theatre.'

'Well as long as I get paid for this extra hour at the theatre,' ventured Albert.

That wiped the smile from the Mayor's face. 'Albert,' the Mayor said gruffly. 'Haven't I explained this to you enough times? We split the profits. It's a cooperative, remember.'

'Did you read that in the Gigot County Bulletin as well?'

'Let me remind you that you'll be the last to complain if at six o'clock every night everyone is throwing money at us like confetti? It's called free enterprise.'

'I thought you said it was a cooperative.'

'It's both. We have the right to make money without state interference. And the right to share the money equally among the employees. In my mind that seems fair. So you can moan and you can gripe and you can stand there as long as you like. But you're not going to get anything.'

Albert was about to say something incredibly cutting and harsh concerning the Mayor's estranged son and ex-wife when Miss Murs started yelling hysterically from the first-floor window she'd been looking out of for the past hour.

'Everyone! There are people coming down the hill from the bypass.'

'Right,' boomed Jean Marc almost standing to attention himself. 'Miss Murs, when we're full in here, I'll direct them to you - you're *Le Overflow* remember. Very important.'

'Great!' squeaked Miss Murs and disappeared inside.

Jean Marc glared at Albert. 'Get inside,' he ordered as the rain started to slash down. 'And get your apron on. It's time to work.'

The maintenance mumbled something like. 'Fuck you, you old bastard.' But the Mayor chose not to hear it.

'Madame Coquelicot,' Jean Marc instead called out. 'Skillet on? Steaks ready? Chips?'

The old woman nodded while wiping grease all over her velvet dress as she refused point-blank to wear an apron, claiming it made her look like a common garden cook.

'Francis, wine uncorked?' barked the Mayor. 'Glasses shined?'

The old drunk nodded.

'Good,' beamed the Mayor. 'As you know, Miss Murs is on standby in her house, which we've called *Le Overflow*. When it gets full in here, I'll send them over there. Are we all ready?'

'Yes, but while I remember,' said Francis whipping a corkscrew out of his pocket like a knife and uncorking a bottle in double quick time. 'What actually is your role here? I mean while we slog our asses off serving and pouring drinks. What do you actually do?'

Murmurs of approval all round.

Jean Marc cursed them all. 'I'm the Mayor, Francis, the face of the community, and my job is meeting and greeting people. You don't expect me to get my hands dirty, do you?'

Francis nearly fell forwards into the bar. 'Hell no,' he roared. 'Miracles might happen. God might even exist. But Jean Marc Bulot get his hands dirty? Never!'

'Francis,' expounded Jean Marc. 'Someone has to look the part. Someone has to be front-of-house. Clean cut. It's part of the image. Who goes into a restaurant and is greeted by the chef with half a carcass over his shoulder?'

‘The Japanese do,’ declared Albert tucking a tea towel into his stiffly starched apron. ‘Apparently a Japanese chef will present guests with what he’s going to cook for them before they eat it.'

‘Not sure there’s room for a horse in here,’ howled Francis.

Jean Marc nearly had a fit. ‘We don’t serve horse, Francis.’

‘It’s not what Madame Coquelicot told me,’ Francis replied.

‘Madame Coquelicot wouldn’t know a rabbit from a giraffe.'

'Shall we ask her?' asked Francis.

'No, we shall not ask her...' Jean Marc’s voice tailed off as he saw a large-headed woman standing in front of him dripping wet.

'*Bonsoir, Madame,*' he greeted her praying she didn't understand French. But just in case: 'Our waiter here Francis was just telling us about how he loves riding horses on a Sunday morning,' Jean Marc quickly rattled off in French.

'I'm sorry. I don't understand. I don't speak French,' she said looking at the short squat figure of Francis Conda dressed in a white tuxedo too small for him, his long beard tucked into the inside of his lapel like a serviette. Even if she had understood, she wouldn't have believed him.

'Oh I'm sorry,' said Jean Marc in English, mightily relieved. 'How can we help you?'

'Do you serve Crêpes?' asked the woman bluntly.

‘Err, I’m sorry,' he answered. 'Just *beef* steak and frites.' He emphasized the word, beef.

‘But it says *Place de Crêpe*?' she said pointing outside to the sign in the village square which was now an ocean of pure silver in the pouring rain.

‘Ah,’ said the Mayor realising the confusion, ‘that refers to the village square. The village is called Crêpe.’

‘Really?’ exclaimed the woman. ‘I didn’t see a sign. I thought we were in Ventrèche.’

'Sorry about that. Our maintenance man will be rectifying that tomorrow. Madame, how many are there?' The Mayor looked beyond the woman towards the door.

'I'm sorry but we won't be staying.’

‘Oh.’ The Mayor looked like he was definitely about to cry this time.

‘We're vegetarian you see...’

The word vegetarian knifed Jean Marc in the back.

'...That’s why we were hoping for a Crêpe. A lovely cheese Crêpe or one with sugar and lemon sprinkled on it. But if you’ve got nothing vegetarian then we’ll be going, especially as we’re soaking wet.’

And then in a single motion the knife was painlessly withdrawn and for the second time that year he had another piano-falling-on-his-head idea.

In his previous life as a jobbing, not particularly busy, mayor of a small-time village, one of the highlights of the year was waiting for Lent to come round. Those early spring days when Miss Murs used to bring him a steaming plate of pancakes, lemon juice and honey into his office. Jean Marc had never been the most complimentary mayor in the world, but he had always congratulated her on her Crêpes. ‘Miss Murs I doubt there’s anybody in France who can cook Crêpes as well as you,’ he had often simpered.

'Of course we serve Crêpes,’ the Mayor proclaimed to the woman. ‘Our Crêperie is just next door. If you give me a minute, I'll check we’re ready.'

And with that Jean Marc pelted it to Miss Murs’ house.

'Miss Murs, we need some Crêpes making pronto,’ he spluttered, skimming water off his suit jacket onto her newly polished kitchen floor. 'Family of English vegetarians - rabbit feeders, no meat, not even bits of ham. You know how fussy they are, totally destroyed the art of cooking. Pain in the ass they are - I should have them shot.'

'I'm vegetarian,' stated Miss Murs quietly.

'Really?' said Jean Marc as the cartoon character of Jean Marc Bulot broke into small bits and crashed to the floor. 'I never knew that.'

'You never asked.'

'How did you cope growing up?'

'My parents were vegetarian and my grandparents before that. Runs in the family.'

In the fifty years since school, Jean Marc had learnt little new. Almost nothing in fact. Even the simple news that his next door neighbour and work colleague was vegetarian had completely passed him by. Of course it wasn't his fault; he had never had dinner or lunch with her. Like most in rural France, people were obsessively private about their eating habits so perhaps there was no reason to know. Yet on the other hand maybe he should have known. He had known her all his life, since she was a baby. She had been the village secretary for thirty years. Furthermore, she was a vegetarian in a village where most people weren't. It made him wonder how much other knowledge, however small or insignificant, he had missed out on over the years, simply by not listening or not being interested - probably quite a lot.

'I'm sorry, I didn't know,' he admitted sheepishly.

'It's fine, I would eat meat, only I can't digest it - some weird family genetic disease that renders the stomach unable to digest flesh. If I eat it, it just stays in my stomach and I have to be sick. It's horrible actually.'

Jean Marc felt better and rushed back to the Town Hall to inform the waiting family that Crêpes were being served next door if they would like to follow him.

Chapter 12 - Le Camping

Opening *La Crêperie* - as *Le Overflow* was quickly renamed - was a masterstroke. Eggs and flour were cheap and no one could rival Miss Murs' culinary expertise when it came to the Crêpe. Not that Jean Marc was going to let her take much of the credit.

'If I had my day again Albert,' he blathered on at the end of service a week later, 'I could rival the guy who set up McDonald's. BULOTS I would call it, or maybe King of the Crêpe, available in two hundred countries, 32,000 restaurants with me, the founder and Chief Executive, Jean Marc Bulot, sitting in his high castle in the Swiss Alps. Imagine that Albert.'

But Albert wasn't listening. He was busy folding napkins into any shape that came to mind. A seagull, a fish, a diamond, a star, a fan, simply to keep himself awake. Albert Gramme was exhausted. He had never worked so hard in his life and was realising what real work was really like. Being the village maintenance man in a village where no one lived or ever visited was comparable to fighting a war against an enemy that didn't exist. Which was why he'd spent most of his working life sharpening tools in the maintenance hut by the stadium, just in case. A long way from where he thought he might be when he was growing up.

Like many teenage boys he wanted to play guitar, form a band, be famous, get laid and leave Crêpe. But at forty-three - and still the second youngest member of the village after Bernard Cle's grandson - Albert Gramme hadn't left Crêpe, hadn't formed a band, wasn't famous and hadn't got laid, although he could play guitar, but not very well. Mainly because he spent his free time watching music videos on satellite TV in the house of his dead parents, who'd gassed themselves one Christmas Eve when the strain of living became too much.

They'd actually intended to take the young fifteen-year-old Albert with them, but by sheer luck he had snuck out that night with his friend Alain Dupain to watch a Def Leppard gig in Gigot. He survived, and from that day on always wore Def Leppard T-shirts as a token to his good fortune.

'Our problem, Albert,' the Mayor droned on. 'Is the lack of space. Look outside, it's like a bloody service station. All those ghastly oversized motorhomes with their panoramic windscreens. They're so ugly, I wish we could have them out of sight.'

'How about the old Guesthouse?' suggested Albert warily. 'We could bulldoze it and make it into a car park.'

'It's a listed building believe it or not.'

'How about converting the football pitch into a campsite? We could use the old changing rooms as a toilet block. Use my hut as a reception. It wouldn't take much to bring it up to scratch. Mow the grass, paint the walls.'

Jean Marc stared at a napkin in the shape of a guitar. 'Bloody hell Albert, that's a brilliant idea. I can't believe I didn't think of that myself.'

'It would be perfect,' carried on Albert feeling enthusiastic someone had listened to one of his ideas. 'It's only a stone's throw away from the square.'

'We could even get a football team together. Relive the glory days of *L'equipe de Crêpe*,' Jean Marc reminisced his face becoming bright red.

Albert's head dropped. If there was one thing he hated more than folding napkins, jazz music and spicy food, it was listening to the Mayor talk about football. Unfortunately, he had the feeling, as he finished folding his one thousandth napkin of the day, this time in the shape of a trapezium, that he was about to hear the Crêpe Football Story once again.

In 1967, Jean Marc, then a sinewy seventeen-year-old, played for Crêpe in the Gigot regional cup final against Ventrèche. They met in the local league twice a year, but this was the first time they'd played each other in the cup final, which that year, was scheduled to be played at the *Stade de Crêpe* on 31st May 1967.

Even before the demise of Crêpe there had always been an unhealthy animosity between the two villages. Some say it started during the war when Ventrèche supported the Germans and Crêpe resisted them. Many however thought it went back further, to the Middle Ages, old family feuds that were unresolved and left to linger and fester for centuries, creating hate and suspicion. The infamous cup final of 1967 encapsulated five hundred years of hate in one violent ninety minutes.

Within seconds of kickoff, Jean Marc, playing centre forward, felt the sharp studs of Fabian "Boots" Quesnoys rake down the back of his calf sending him to the floor in agony. In any other game he would have been stretchered off and gone straight to hospital. But not this game. This wasn't a game to cry off injured, go home crying to *maman* for a glass of milk. This was a battle. Jean Marc gritted his teeth, bit his tongue and played on until the bitter end, during which he was hacked, elbowed, punched with every run he made.

It wasn't in vain though, he scored twice, and with the match at two-all heading into extra time Crêpe had their tails up. Ventrèche were ragged, tired and unfit. Too many late, boozy, cigarettey nights were taking their toll. The game was there to be won; Jean Marc could sense it.

Then disaster struck. Two minutes before the end Ventrèche's all-star winger Jacques "The Ballerina" Breton, who had once had trials with Olympique Lyonnais, cut in from the right and drove toward Crêpe's goal. On seeing a wall of impenetrable Crêpe defenders Breton threw himself into midair, performed a perfect swallow dive and hit the ground like he'd been machine-gunned.

Jean Marc often frowned at the theatrical antics of today's footballers when he watched them on TV. But they paled into insignificance compared to Jacques Breton's tumble. Crêpe's defenders cleared the ball high into the stand and were expecting a throw-in. Surely even this ref, who had displayed a sickening bias against Crêpe throughout the match, wouldn't be conned by Breton's pantomime dive. But they were left swallowing their tongues and gasping for air when the referee pointed to the spot. He could have been forgiven if he was still puffing in the centre circle and struggling to keep up, but he wasn't. He was standing right next to Breton when he went down. Practically holding his hand.

It didn't take long for the ensuing melee between the players on the field to quickly escalate into a full-scale riot involving everyone, players, managers and the crowd alike. Players were beaten, spectators mauled, half the stand was smashed up, and the referee had to take cover in his car until the pitch was deemed safe enough for him to return.

After a lengthy delay, Frederick "The Hammer" Lacombe, blasted the ball home from the spot kick, giving Ventrèche a 3-2 lead. The referee immediately blew his whistle (even though, according to Crêpe's manager Gilles "Gitane" Petard, who later attacked Ventrèche's manager Alain "Gaulois" Pelle with a Kronenbourg bottle, there were eight minutes left to play) and Ventrèche won the match.

There was more violence afterwards and as a result both teams were banned from the following year's competition and fined three hundred Francs. Crêpe never won the cup and in 1998 the team was disbanded leaving the old stadium and pitch to rust and decay.

'After the match,' Jean Marc recalled, now nearing the end of his story, 'I went to the far edge of the field to vomit and lick my wounds. Then before anyone could find me, I took a shortcut home and stayed in bed for a week, refusing to get up. I didn't attend the end of season awards despite getting Player of the Year. I gave my bottle of Champagne to my mother. I've actually still got it, it's probably worth a fortune by now. Or sour.'

He let the word sour linger in the room for a few moments before Albert made his retort, now on napkin #1320: 'So Francis was right, JM. This isn't about making Crêpe great again, is it? Not at all. It's all about getting one over Ventrèche for a football match that was played over fifty years ago.'

Jean Marc was going to deny it, but changed his mind. 'Yes. I'll admit it Albert.'

'Thought so.'

'However, the fact remains Albert, we've been living in Ventrèche's shadow for far too long. It's time to step out of it now we've been given this glorious opportunity. We must use it and if it crushes Ventrèche in the process, even better,' finished Jean Marc, picking up an olive from a bowl and crushing it in his fingers, the green flesh exploding out onto the floor.

'So tomorrow, find that mower and make that football field as smooth as it was in 1967, so when those campers pitch up it feels like they're pitching up on Wembley stadium,' the Mayor proclaimed proudly.

'The grass is probably a mile high by now.'

'Find a scythe or a pair of shears then. By tonight I want to be able to putt a golf ball from the centre circle to the penalty spot.'

'And also Albert,' added Jean Marc. 'Tomorrow could you please find that damn village sign and put it back up. I'm sick of people arriving and thinking they are in Ventrèche.'

'But there is no village sign,' replied Albert solemnly. 'Don't you remember? It was taken down by the construction company when they built the new road and never put back.'

'Really?' Jean Marc looked towards the bypass in disbelief. 'But that was over fifteen years ago. Are you telling me there hasn't been a village sign for fifteen years?'

'I can order one from the Gigot County Public Works if you want,' offered Albert.

'Forget it. It would take another fifteen years to arrive and then it would probably be spelt wrong. Just paint one on a piece of wood or something. Anything, so long as it says CRÊPE on it big and bold.'

'I can paint angels on it if you like?' grinned the maintenance man.

Jean Marc frowned. 'That won't be necessary, Albert. We've got enough religious iconography on that sodding tower,' protested the Mayor pointing to the gargoyles, cherubim and seraphim crowding the church tower. 'Which reminds me, have you sorted those bells out yet?'

Albert sighed. 'I'll do it tomorrow. Anything else? Do you want me to wipe your bottom for you as well?'

Jean Marc winced. 'I think that will be all for now.'

'Can I go home?'

'Yes.'

'Because if I fold another napkin, I think I'll go stark raving mad.' Albert looked at the Mayor with his terrible grin which sent a shiver down Jean Marc's spine.

'Yes,' the Mayor replied suddenly feeling incredibly tired himself. 'You go home. Get some rest. You might need it. It could be a long summer ahead.'

Albert's head dropped. 'I thought so. For a minute, I thought you were going to say we could all go home to bed and forget about this whole stupid charade.'

Jean Marc smiled. 'Sometimes I'd love to. Go back to those lazy days of doing fuck all. Looking out of the window. Waiting for the odd car. Then going back inside for a cup of tea, sitting in front of the TV for five hours straight watching some stupid quiz show. Then a short walk round the square. Then bed.'

The Mayor paused.

'But sometimes Albert, you've got to grab life by the balls even if it means folding napkins.'

Albert was waiting for the second part of Jean Marc's monumental speech. Some grand conclusion as to why they were all here. But it never came. The Mayor simply got up, said good night, and went upstairs to bed. Leaving Albert alone in the dark restaurant to contemplate the sheer meaninglessness of existence.

Chapter 13 - Les Gendarmes

'I miss our lunches back in your old house,' Francis complained to Jean Marc as he doled out a portion of duck for their traditional Saturday lunch a few days into the month of June. 'Feels like we're at work having lunch here.'

'It's too noisy over there now we've got the campsite. Full of drunks rolling back from Bernard's bar after drinking his gut-wrenching wine all night long.'

'How's he getting along with Bar La Boucle?' He took a slug of red Ventoux. 'To be honest I'm surprised he bothered opening that wreck of a place. Thought he would have wanted to reopen his bakery.'

'I mentioned it to him, even gave him good rates on the lease. But he said he was too old to get up at three o'clock every morning.'

Francis accepted the point. 'Hard work running a bar though. I've sat and watched a few bar keepers live and die in my time,' he smiled at Jean Marc.

'He enjoys it,' countered Jean Marc. 'Says he likes the late nights, plus he's learning English. Got a new step in his stride.'

'It's about time,' Francis concluded. 'He's never been the same since his wife left him.'

'Tell me about it. What is it about this place - all the women simply leave.'

Francis nodded. 'It's why I never got married. I knew they would leave so I saved myself the heartbreak.'

'*Monsieur Practical,*' Jean goaded him. 'Work, drink, sleep. The simple life of Francis Conda. No wife, no children, no heartbreak.'

'Talking of romance, how are you and Miss Murs getting on?'

Jean Marc stared back at his friend. 'What on earth are you talking about?'

'When's the wedding?' pressed Francis.

'Don't be ridiculous.'

'You're always looking at her when she's serving.'

'I do no such thing, probably checking she's not sloshing gravy everywhere.'

'Just marry her,' Francis ordered. 'It's no biggie. I mean it's not as though you're going to be stuck with her for fifty years.' He burst out laughing. 'Plus you can die happy knowing she'll be able to pick up your generous La Poste pension instead of her crummy Town Hall one.'

'Why don't you marry her seeing as you've got her interests at heart.'

'Because I don't love her.'

'Nor do I.' His voice became a high-pitched whoop.

Francis beamed to himself, content in his own personal victory over his friend. 'I hear Ethel Budd is reopening the old grocery shop on the square as well.'

'Tesco,' said Jean Marc quickly, glad to change the subject.

'Tesco?'

'It's a supermarket in the UK. Her nephew is buying up stuff from there and bringing it over in a van. British food. Weird stuff. Salty biscuits, flat beer, and something called Marmite - some sort of jam.'

Francis mumbled something but his eyelids were drooping, and soon they were drifting into their afternoon naps.

'Police!' came a cry from downstairs fifteen minutes later.

Jean Marc and Francis woke up and looked at each other as though they were four years old, glued to their soft springless chairs.

'Police,' came the cry again.

'Just a minute,' the Mayor half shouted down wondering why no one else was getting the door. Where the hell was Albert or Miss Murs?

Once Jean Marc had wiped the gravy off his shirt and charged downstairs, he opened the giant door of the Town Hall and saw two identikit Gendarmes fresh out of the academy in Dijon standing in front of him. Pale, black haired, mid-twenties with no discernible features whatsoever apart from a faint moustache and a slight paunch from too many helpings of mummy's pot-au-feu and brie filled baguettes. By forty they would both be bald, fat and look the same as their fathers. At fifty they'd retire and watch Top Pets until they died around sixty-nine.

'Afternoon,' said Jean Marc in English. 'What can I do for you? A bite to eat?'

Their faces went blank. 'Ugh?'

'Sorry,' resumed Jean Marc in French. 'I thought you were customers.'

'That's what we are here to enquire about, Monsieur Bulot, these customers and your restaurants, and the bar and this shop,' said the first one.

'And now a campsite as well,' added the second pointing across the square towards the old stadium.

'Do you have an appointment?' asked Jean Marc. 'I'm very busy. Maybe I'll check with Miss Murs, our secretary, to see if we've got any spaces in our schedule today. Or maybe you're looking for a job?"

'Monsieur Bulot. We don't need appointments and we don't need a job,' continued the first one puffing his pigeon chest out as best he could. 'We're the police in case you hadn't noticed.'

'Naturally,' said Jean Marc ushering them into the building and into his dusty office. 'How can I help you?' he asked closing the door firmly behind them.

'So,' started number one taking out a notepad from his pocket in his perfectly ironed shirt. 'I assume all these new businesses are registered.'

'Of course,' replied Jean Marc a little too quickly. 'Why wouldn't they be?'

'I don't know, Monsieur. Why wouldn't they be?' he repeated. 'That's what we are asking you!'

Jean Marc sighed; disappointed modern police work still seemed to rely on repeating what the suspect had just said in order to generate a negative response so that the dummy Gendarmes felt they had cracked the case. Rather than taking Lieutenant Colombo's line of questioning that might involve asking what recipe Jean Marc used for the steak sauce. Putting the suspect at ease and leading him or her into a false sense of security, therefore increasing the chances the suspect would make a mistake in the future.

But not here. These idiots were showing all their cards at once. If nothing else, it was plain damn lazy police work.

'All tax and social security registered I assume,' they blundered on. 'Proper receipts issued and accounts. Fire, health and safety, kitchen inspection. Not that I'm saying you wouldn't have everything in order of course being the Mayor of such a pleasant place as Crêpe.' Both the policemen sniggered.

'So when you've got a minute Monsieur Bulot, we'll take a quick glance at your documents for each of the businesses registered in the commune of Crêpe. Employee contracts and so forth. And of course, your alcohol and food hygiene licenses and certificates. Plus your permit for changing the use of a public building into a restaurant. I'm sure this used to be the Town Hall?'

Since they'd merged the Crêpe Gendarmerie into the one in Ventrèche fifteen years ago these pie-faced goons standing in front of him had complete jurisdiction in his village and there was nothing he could do about it except shoot them with his father's shotgun he kept in his apartment.

'I'll post them to you next week,' stammered the Mayor trying to keep calm. 'I'm a little busy at the moment.'

'We don't mind waiting,' said the first. 'Got all day in fact. Nothing else to do.'

That he believed. 'Well. It'll take me awhile to gather up all the paperwork. Miss Murs isn't in today and she does all that sort of thing.'

'Oh, I thought you just said Miss Murs could book us in for an appointment today,' queried the first. 'Or did I mishear you.'

This was all spinning out of control and Jean Marc was wondering how much a reasonable bribe was these days, when Miss Murs charged in carrying a file.

'I thought you were taking the day off Miss Murs,' said Jean Marc feigning confusion.

'Oh no, that was yesterday,' she replied quickly understanding the situation. 'I just overheard your conversation - I hope you don't mind - so I quickly got the relevant information together, so as not to waste the Gendarmes' time.'

She politely handed the first Gendarme a manila envelope. 'I know how much the police have got on these days especially with all the spending cuts so I hope everything is in order.'

'Yes,' agreed the first, slightly taken aback. 'That's true. Thank you very much, Miss Murs.' He took the file.

'Very efficient,' said the second disappointedly. 'Not that we had any doubt. Of course.'

'We pride ourselves in Crêpe,' Jean Marc coughed. 'On our commitment to upholding the law where every man has the right to work coupled with the obligation to pay his taxes towards the upkeep of this glorious nation.'

'And as a special treat for our favourite Gendarmes from Ventrèche,' added Miss Murs. 'How about steak-frites and a bottle of Bordeaux on the house?'

'Oh no Madame, we're on duty.'

'Are you sure?' asked Miss Murs.

'We'll be on our way, thank you,' they said edging towards the door. 'It's been another fantastic experience coming to Crêpe, we won't forget it.' And with that they left.

'Phew, that was close,' swooned Miss Murs. 'Why on earth did you let them in?'

'They were banging on the door. Where the hell was everyone else?'

'In the basement hiding.'

'Why?'

'So it looked like no one was in, I sent Albert out to inspect the stadium. You two were meant to be asleep. I knew they were coming you see. I had a tip-off.'

'From whom?'

'My friend Annette is the secretary for the mayor in Ventrèche and she heard the Gendarmes boasting with him the other day that they were going to pay us a visit. She phoned me right away.'

Jean Marc's eyes narrowed. 'Miss Murs I hope you're not sleeping with the enemy? And why didn't you tell me?'

'Because you and Francis always have your Saturday lunch at two o'clock and then sleep, so I thought there was no reason to inform you.'

'Please do it next time, Miss Murs. We both practically had heart attacks when the banging started.'

'OK,' she agreed. 'But Annette told me the Mayor of Ventrèche, your friend Michel Arnold, is getting nervous that we're taking their business, so he was sending over the Gendarmes to scare us.'

'He's not my friend.'

'I thought not. But why did they send over the cops and not the *inspecteur de travail?* Everyone knows they have more power than the rural police over work regulation issues.'

'I agree, Miss Murs. But Monsieur Arnold doesn't want the work inspectors snooping around all the underhand and dodgy businesses in Ventrèche.'

'What a nation we live in where the bureaucrats have more power than the police,' she tutted.

'Blame the socialists,' commented the Mayor.

'I thought you were a Socialist?'

'I'm the Mayor of a small village in the middle of nowhere. It doesn't matter what I am. I'm just here.'

Miss Murs looked rather impressed with his philosophical statement.

'Whose file did you give them anyway?' the Mayor asked, as he was getting ready to go back upstairs.

'Yours.'

'What!' screamed Jean Marc. 'Are you drunk or something, Miss Murs?'

'Oh come on Jean Marc. You saw them when they saw the file, they lost interest. It wouldn't have mattered which file I gave them. I could've given them the Sunday papers from 1987 and they wouldn't have noticed. I just happened to see your file first. And anyway, I wouldn't worry Jean Marc,' she smiled and picked up the file from the desk. 'They didn't even take it.' She held the file up beaming.

'What would have happened if they'd taken it - it's totally fabricated. I haven't paid taxes for years.'

'Then you'd have probably gone to jail,' she said casually.

'Miss Murs, please don't try a stunt like that again. You've done brilliantly, but next time give them Albert's file. Bizarre as it may sound, he's the only person in the village who doesn't lie on his tax form. Which reminds me that I must tell him not to be so honest this year, otherwise we are screwed. I don't want Albert Gramme to be the smoking gun.'

'Maybe he could be the one to take the rap for all of us if it all goes wrong,' Miss Murs suggested mischievously.

'Miss Murs,' he scolded her gently. 'Albert Gramme has never hurt anyone in his life. But yes, I think that's a great idea.'

They both laughed while they watched the poor maintenance wander across the village square with a scythe.

Jean Marc was about to walk out of the office when he did something he had never done before. He kissed her. It was only a peck on the cheek, but a kiss is a kiss. He then bounded upstairs to his apartment taking two steps at a time with the thought that for the first time in over forty years he might be in love.

Chapter 14 - Michel Arnold

When Jean Marc received his first pay check at the age of seventeen, he went straight to the travel agent in Gigot, to ask how much a trip to Hawaii cost.

The severely dressed woman looked him up and down with grey steely eyes, her brilliantly dyed, permed and quaffed hair glowing in the bright florescent lights as though it was about to catch on fire. She looked at her colleague in the next booth, who was also eyeing up the lanky kid in his freshly pressed La Poste uniform. She slowly turned her head round to face Jean Marc, a tiny glob of spittle coated in pink lipstick resting on her thick bottom lip.

‘Postmen don't go to Hawaii,' she cruelly attested. 'You might get to Biarritz if you're lucky.'

Jean Marc turned around and marched himself out of the travel agent, took the bus back to his parents' house by the stadium and went to bed without food or water for a week.

He had thought about that moment almost as much as Jacques Breton's swallow dive, and now with money in the bank - or at least in his attic - his dream of going to Hawaii was near. Nothing was going to stop him, especially not Michel Arnold and his dodgy cops.

'Jean Marc!' It was Miss Murs shouting from below. Her voice mixed with panic.

'The Mayor of Ventrèche is here to see you.'

But Jean Marc already knew this because he'd seen his stupid American Buick pull up. He wasn't surprised either. Sooner or later the wretched man was bound to make an appearance.

Two minutes later Jean Marc was downstairs. 'Thank you Miss Murs, that will be all.' He didn't like to exclude her, but this was personal.

Michel Arnold was dressed in a Stetson and a brown nylon shirt with elephants on it. His jeans were too tight round his fatty waist, which hung over his buffalo skin belt like a half-inflated balloon.

'Bonjour, Jean Marc,' he said as he boldly walked into the office and stood upright by the door.

'I'm sorry but as I told your Gendarmes last week, we have an appointment system for visitors from another village,' Jean Marc looked directly into the heavily bloodshot eyes of his archenemy. Clearly another night on the pastis.

'I was thinking of trying your restaurant out.'

'Sorry but we're not open yet.'

Michel looked at his watch. 'Bloody hell Jean Marc, it's one o'clock.'

'And?'

'But it's lunchtime.'

'We don't do lunch.'

The Mayor of Ventrèche let out a small stunted laugh, emitting just enough air to blow a fly from the end of a pencil. 'You don't do lunch? We are in France you know. Or hadn't you noticed?'

'I'm not catering for the French,' Jean Marc replied emphatically. 'I'm catering for the British, and they don't do lunch like we do; they prefer to stick to sandwiches and eat a proper meal in the evening. And quite frankly, I agree with them.'

'Never a patriot, were you Bulot?'

'I'm a businessman first. A patriot second,' Jean Marc stated firmly as though he had been rehearsing those lines for decades.

Michel laughed again. 'Oh God this is good. Retired postman and village Mayor becomes highflyer tycoon overnight.'

'I'm glad you find it all so funny Michel.'

'What's funnier is that rumour has it you're going to Hawaii.'

'Rumours are rumours.'

'Yes, I suppose they are. Especially as Hawaii is a long way from Biarritz. For a postman anyway.'

'How's business in Ventrèche?' asked Jean Marc ignoring him.

'You should come and have a look one day for yourself.'

'I'd rather shoot myself.'

'Very confident talk Jean Marc, good to see you haven't lost your swagger.'

'I never had one.'

'I've always admired your humour.'

'Is there a reason for your visit Michel, or are you here to simply force me to hit you?'

'I don't think that'll be necessary, between friends.'

'We're not friends Michel.'

'Violette left and went to live in Ventrèche on her own accord.'

Jean Marc said nothing.

'And it wasn't my decision to close La Poste in Crêpe either.'

'You were the regional director at the time. It had to be you.'

'Orders from above. I tried to save it - it's on the record if you insist - but I was out voted. There was nothing I could do about it.'

‘I lost my job because of that.’

‘Rubbish Jean Marc. You were offered a nice retirement package, or the option to work in Ventrèche. You chose retirement. And now you're Mayor and have a nice apartment and you still have your house by the stadium. So don’t give me that crap.’

‘I was fifty-two. I wasn’t ready to hang up my bag or put away my bicycle, but what choice did I have. I couldn’t come and live in Ventrèche. I would have been a laughing stock.’

Michel shrugged.

‘Retirement was hard. I used to crucify myself daily watching the new postmen zoom in and out in their banana yellow Citroen Berlingos, radios blaring. Delivering the mail as quickly as possible without a word to anyone. Not even a customary hello. I was devastated. For thirty-four years I did that job with pride and distinction. Only to see the job I loved reduced to a mere mechanical procedure. A job no more interesting than gutting fish.’

‘We have to move with the times, Jean Marc. And anyway, I didn’t come here to discuss the past, I came here to settle a few scores.'

‘Ah, I understand what this is about. Now the shoe is on the other foot you’ve come crawling back here. I wonder why that is Michel? Business bad in Ventrèche is it?'

‘Business in Ventrèche is booming.’

Jean Marc could tell by the way the Mayor of Ventrèche had started fiddling with his ridiculous string tie he was lying out of his arse.

‘So why are you here then?’

‘I’m just curious how you managed to turn a wreck of a village into a truck stop?’

'That's well put, I like that. Well at least our truck stop is full.'

'How did you do it Jean Marc?'

'Charisma,' Jean Marc boasted.

'Hardly. Or is there something else you're not sharing Jean Marc? Some mysterious Glitch?'

Jean Marc shot up in his chair: 'How do you know about that?'

'So it's true,' smiled Michel Arnold.

Jean Marc was seething. The conniving runt of a man had caught him off guard. 'I don't know what you're talking about.'

'I've heard the rumours, something to do with dodgy satnavs rerouting cars and campers through Crêpe instead of Ventrèche. Come on it's hardly a military secret. Probably happens all the time.'

'Well maybe you should wait for your turn then,' Jean Marc shouted back, sounding like a child.

'Oh come on Jean Marc, we've known each other all our lives. Yes, we've had some ups and downs but isn't it true that most Frenchmen can't stand the sight of each other? I mean look at you and Francis Conda and Bernard. You argue all the time. It's part of our culture.'

'You're lucky Francis isn't here; he'd probably kill you.'

'I'm not scared of that clown Conda. I'm surprised he's still alive.'

'Say that to his face then - he should be here soon.'

Michel edged a fraction towards the door.

'Plus there's another rumour going round Ventrèche that you and Miss Murs are very close.'

Jean Marc gave a long drawn out 'Ahhh. So that's it, isn't it?' The Mayor was almost laughing. 'That's why you've come all the way over here dressed in your ridiculous cowboy getup. Violette's got you right under the thumb, hasn't she? Sending you out here to hoover up some gossip so she's got something to talk about in the hairdressers. Life in Ventrèche must be really exciting. Before you know it, it'll be all around the butcher, the baker and the candlestick maker. By which time we'll be getting married.'

'It's true then?'

'Don't be ridiculous Arnold. We're professional round here, we don't lure women here with the promise of trips to the Bronco.'

'She came to me Jean Marc.'

'Well she must have been blinded by something. Probably the dazzle from your bald patch.'

Jean Marc ran his hand through his thick strong hair, which had only greyed in the last ten years, then looked back at Michel Arnold. Once a fit, strong, young athletic man, now he was a fat knackered pig. Too many long lunches, cigars and bottles of claret. Jean Marc might not have much, but he had youth on his side. Even at sixty-seven he could pelt up and down the steep rickety stairs of the Town Hall like a whippet with mustard up its ass. Michel would probably need three stops at least, and even then, he'd probably collapse at the top needing an oxygen mask.

'I've got things to do, Michel. So you go can go back to Ventrèche and inform your lovely wife that unfortunately she'll have to get her gossip from somewhere else. Try the bins, there might be some old magazines covered in piss and shit you can both read?'

Michel Arnold frowned. 'You can be a nasty bastard sometimes. And to think I was coming here thinking we might be friends.'

'Ha!' exploded the Mayor. 'In another life, yes. But not in this one. Now if you'll excuse me, I'm rather busy.' He got up from his desk and opened the door trying as hard as possible not to smash the thick oak panel into his adversary's head.

'It won't last forever Jean Marc.' Michel Arnold aimed the pointed brim of his Stetson towards the open door and walked through it. 'One day this Glitch or whatever it is will go back to normal and Crêpe will sink back into the quicksand of filth and decay where it belongs.'

'Maybe you're mixing up Ventrèche with Crêpe again.'

'Ha ha ha, always one for the wisecrack. Never lose your sense of humour Jean Marc, it's the only thing you've got.'

'Piss off you fat fuck, if you want to fight I'm ready whenever you are. And by the way, in case you haven't noticed, we're not in Tennessee Michel, we're in the middle of shitty rural France. You should take a look around some time, open your eyes.'

'Oh my eyes are open, don't you worry about that.' He let out a rasping laugh wafting the aroma of his half-digested lunch over Jean Marc. Snails, garlic, pate, sausage taken with a bottle of cheap rose.

'My eyes are wide open and all I can see is a Frenchman in a stupid Stetson. Please don't come here again.'

'Or what Jean Marc?' Michel cut in. 'You'll set Miss Murs on me, or that drunk Francis. Or that retard Albert. Or maybe I'll get hit over the head by Madame Coquelicot. Ha! Clowns, you all are,' he said just as a hot faced Albert Gramme charged in carrying a scythe.

'Oh, morning Albert,' Michel quivered as he looked into Albert's sunken eyes.

'What do you want?' Albert demanded.

'Oh nothing.' And Michel Arnold quickly skipped to his car.

'What did he want?'

'Nothing,' the Mayor smiled. 'I think he's getting a touch concerned we're taking his business. But don't worry, they won't stop Crêpe now.'

'Well they will if the punters can't enter the village.'

'What!'

'Someone's blocked the road. Ethel Budd's nephew just tried to come down it in his van from the bypass, but there's two Gendarmes blocking it with barriers.'

'Shit!'

Chapter 15 - A Barrier to Progress

'I knew that creepy bastard was up to something,' cursed Jean Marc as he cycled frantically down the hill from Crêpe with Albert behind on his ancient Peugeot PK10. 'I should have known he simply came to distract me.'

'The nephew had to go all the way back to Ventrèche and round. Ethel Budd was fuming.'

'I'm not surprised,' snorted Jean Marc as they approached the bottom of the hill and crossed the stream that gave Crêpe its name: Le Crêpe.

'Never trust a man wearing a hat,' advised Jean Marc as they puffed their way up the other side of the hill towards the bypass.

'How about a beret?' asked Albert, struggling to keep up with the Mayor's stiff pace.

'Have you ever seen anyone in Crêpe wear a beret?' Jean Marc shouted back over his shoulder.

'No,' wheezed Albert. 'Oh hang on. Mayor Lafarge did.'

'Which proves my point entirely. All crooks,' he said loudly as they rounded the hill and approached the same two dopey policemen who'd visited him a few weeks ago, both standing gormlessly in front of two barricades blocking the road to Crêpe.

'Expecting anyone important?' Jean Marc quipped as he pulled up in front of them. 'Papal visit? President on his way, is he?'

'Orders,' said the first policeman.

'I wasn't informed,' replied Jean Marc trying to keep calm once again.

'Your road is unsafe, you don't need to be informed,' said the second.

'What's unsafe about it?'

'Yeh,' coughed Albert when he finally arrived. 'Looks fine to me, you could roll a bowling ball down it.'

Jean Marc looked back along the perfectly level tarmacked road. Albert was right, he could make a perfect strike into the heart of the village.

'The road is unsafe,' the second repeated. 'That's all you need to know Albert Gramme, so best you get back home.'

'This is bullshit. Who put you up to his?' Jean Marc blasted.

'Orders,' stated the first.

'From whom?'

'That's none of your business.'

'Blocking my village is very much my business.' He shoved past them towards the first barrier. 'Albert, give us a hand to move these.'

'Certainly,' said the maintenance man.

'Monsieur,' the first policeman said. 'You're obstructing police business.'

'This is my business,' Jean Marc snarled, grabbing the tinny and cheap corrugated metal barriers that were probably bought on Michel Arnold's credit card from Pole Vert. 'This is my village!'

'If you continue to do that, we'll arrest both of you,' declared the second policeman.

'Arrest us then,' snapped Jean Marc. 'We'll take the flak. But I tell you, you two are going to look pretty stupid when I stand up in court and tell the jury you were blocking a perfectly good road for no reason whatsoever on the orders of the Mayor who technically has no power over the police. Go on, put the cuffs on if you feel lucky.' He was trying to remember the line from the Dirty Harry film but couldn't.

'How much is Michel Arnold paying you anyway? 100? 150? 200?'

The second Gendarme had the look of a dog caught pissing on the wheel of his owner's car. 'I've no idea what you're talking about,' he retorted.

'Monsieur Bulot,' said the first. 'Are you suggesting we take bribes?'

'I'm not suggesting anything. Just asking a question? Bribe? I didn't mention a bribe. Albert, did I mention a bribe?'

The first policeman's eyes narrowed. Almost reptilian in function: small and jellylike, like a pickled onion, with fragile eyelids half closed over them. 'Well, I think it's nearly lunchtime,' he finally said taking the barrier from Jean Marc. Then stumbled and dropped it making the whole scene look as amateurish and as ridiculous as only rural affairs can be.

Jean Marc decided it was time to take the elder statesman role. 'Look boys, we're all trying to make a stab of it here. We've all taken a few quid under the table in our time or done stuff we shouldn't. There's no harm in that up to a point, but just make sure you know that whoever you are working for knows what they're doing. Otherwise you're going to end up in the merde.

'You may think I'm an old duffer on the postal service retirement gravy train living out my days reminiscing about younger days delivering letters. And you're right. Sometimes I even look at my stamp collection. I'm a sad old fart I know.

'But one thing I do know. This is my village and I'm going to defend it, so you can tell that cocksucking Mayor of yours that he'll have to do better than sending a couple of off-duty cops like you to stop me. Haul me in and charge me, or go home to your lovely Cassoulet I'm sure maman will be cooking you.'

The first one looked like he was going to say something tough but backed down when he saw Albert's menacing eyes scything straight through him. They weren't scared of the Mayor in the slightest. He looked like a grandpa you could knock down with a small stick. Albert on the other hand would need a stake through the heart and a string of garlic the length of the Versailles lawn to kill him. Even with the aid of two loaded guns it would be fifty-fifty against such a rabid beast as Albert Gramme.

'And one final thing,' added Jean Marc. 'If you pull another childish playground stunt like that, I might seriously consider reporting you to the prefecture. And then there will be trouble.'

And with that the Mayor and Albert turned their cycles towards the village and pedalled home leaving the two Policemen quivering with fear.

Excessive violence towards man and beast didn't make the rural folk of Gigot county bat an eyelid. No one was going to lose too much sleep slaughtering a newborn lamb with a blunt knife and watching it die slowly.

But mention The Prefecture, that gothic stone and marble building in the heart of Gigot, and they'd be up till dawn shitting themselves. For the half-witted at least. Jean Marc couldn't give a toss about the prefecture. For him it was a place of laziness, excess, waste and long lunches. Where meetings drew on for days about car parking and porridge shortages. All while gigantic plates of food and carafes of good wine were brought up as though they were re-enacting the treaty of Rome.

Hence why Jean Marc firmly believed in keeping the profits inside his own village. Or preferably, inside his own pocket.

Chapter 16 - Violette Canet-Bulot-Arnold

When Jean Marc turned sixty-seven last year, he thought he'd be lucky to make seventy. Die from the mental turmoil of thinking about all the things he should have done in his life but hadn't.

'Once a postman always a postman,' Francis had goaded him on his first day.

Jean Marc had laughed it off. 'Just a few years Francis saving up a few Francs then I'll be travelling the world living the dream like Ernest Hemingway. Paris, London, Nice, Berlin, Moscow beckons. International jetsetter, entrepreneur, playboy extraordinaire...'

When Jean Marc retired from La Poste, aged fifty-two, he hadn't been anywhere. Hadn't seen the sea. Hadn't seen the Alps. Hadn't left France.

And yet despite all his regrets, at this moment in time he wouldn't change it for the world. Which was why he was considering asking Miss Murs to marry him. An act which, had he been told about six months ago, he would have laughed himself out of the village and died a horrible death in a hedge on the outskirts of Plante.

Plante: regarded by most to be the drabbest village in the province. So drab in fact that almost no one lived there except a crazed Irish doctor who was convinced there was a vat of oil down there the size of Canada. His real name was

Arthur Canne but people called him Jean de Florette after the Gerard Depardieu character in the film of the same name. One because he looked like him and two because he had dug over thirty experimental boreholes all-round the village in his crazed attempt to find the oil which simply wasn't there. There were so many holes scattered around the perimeter that at any minute the entire village would crumble into the ground taking Arthur Canne and everything around him with it.

And yet now Jean Marc was revving himself up for another stab at married life. The turnaround had been remarkable. There was of course the real possibility Miss Murs could say no. But what was there to lose? A bit of face for sure, mild embarrassment and humiliation. But he'd survive. It had happened before. This was Crêpe. Things would go on. They always had. The tractor wheels would turn, the seeds would be sown, the plants would grow, Francis would get drunk and life would go on, marriage or no marriage, Glitch or no Glitch. The sun would fall and rise and another day would start.

He was so excited by the prospect that he was just about to go downstairs, splash himself down with some Korus his son Jacques had bought him on his 50th birthday, and propose right away, when who should turn up but the mother of his errant son.

'Merde,' he cursed. 'What on earth does she want?' And charged downstairs.

'Violette!' he hollered to her outside the Town Hall. 'What a surprise. Let's go for a drink at Bernard's. I'm buying.'

Violette looked totally shocked seeing her ex-husband charge out of the Town Hall like he had been possessed. 'Hi JM.'

'He's reopened Bar La Boucle you know.'

‘Yes, I heard.’

'Come on,' he said grabbing her arm and frog marching her towards Bar La Boucle to the right of the square. 'Bloody hell Jean Marc. Why the rush, you trying to hide me or something?'

'Hide from whom?'

'I don't know, you seem in a terrible rush.'

'I'm always in a rush, didn't you know?'

'I've not come to raid your safe.'

'There is no safe,' corrected Jean Marc looking back over his shoulder to check Miss Murs wasn't curtain twitching. 'Why does everybody think there's a safe?’

‘There’s always a safe isn’t there?’

‘Not here,’ he confirmed as they entered the bar and walked onto the beer-soaked floorboards of Bar La Boucle.

'Bernard!’ Jean Marc ordered. ‘Two glasses of Beaujolais. In fact, forget that, bring the bottle.'

‘Righto,’ said Bernard in English. Bernard’s large oblong head and handlebar moustache made him look like a character from some obscure Mexican graphic novel.

‘Why is he speaking English?’

‘He’s in training - everybody who works for CCC needs to speak English.’

‘What’s CCC?’

‘The Crêpe Catering Committee. It’s the umbrella organisation for the Le Restaurant, La Crêperie, Bar La Boucle and Ethel Budd’s shop. Although technically Ethel Budd is only a non-executive member as she owns her own premises and so controls her own prices - which are extortionate I have to add. Whereas the rest of us in true cooperative style share the profits.’

‘That’s very progressive,’ she commented.

‘Although we struggle like everyone else,’ shrugged Bernard bringing the wine. ‘I mean it’s so difficult to make a living with all the taxes in this country.' Then winked at her knowingly.

Violette nodded in vague agreement and took a sip of wine, screwing up her face like she had been stung by a wasp. 'Bloody hell Bernard, what's this, petrol? Are you trying to poison me?'

'That's my best seller.'

'No wonder you're making money. It's probably cheaper than water.'

Bernard kept a straight face.

'You could have brought us something decent Bernard, I did sit next to you in school for nearly eight years.'

'That's only because your surname was Canet. If that boy Isaac Caan hadn't died in that horrible car crash, you would have had to sit next to him.' Bernard pointed to Jean Marc. 'And I would have had to sit next to Francis. And God knows what would have happened then.'

'I probably wouldn't have married him,' concluded Violette.

'Done us both a favour,' Jean Marc mumbled into his drink.

'I heard that,' she said taking another sip. 'God, tastes like Devil's piss.'

'Best we've got,' declared Bernard. 'You should try the other stuff. Even Francis won't drink it.'

'Anyway,' said Jean Marc shooing Bernard away with his left hand. 'What's with the visit, Violette? Social or business?'

'Both. Michel doesn't know I'm here by the way.'

'I thought he kept tabs on everyone - including his Gendarmes.'

'He does, but he's gone hunting boar.'

'Boar! But it's not the season - it's the middle of summer.'

'Apparently there's a huge beast ripping up someone's sunflower fields, so they have special dispensation to shoot it.'

'Christ, who's he gone with. I hope not those dumb Gendarmes.'

A weak smile spread over Violette's face confirming the nightmarish scenario being played out in Jean Marc's head and indeed on the fields of France. 'Jesus Lord,' hailed Jean Marc. 'It'll be a bloodbath, anyone in the vicinity, walkers, mushroom pickers, even light aircraft will be shot down. The only thing that will live will be the boar.'

Violette giggled. 'You're right, Michel's always complaining about his eyesight, but he's too vain to wear glasses.'

'I should phone the Crime Squad and have them shot on the spot as a danger to national security.'

She smirked and took out a pack of cigarettes, the old nicotine monster still at work, her once pale smooth face now cracked from a life of boozing, fagging and talking. But there was still a pull. That old lust he'd had when he was seventeen, that first dance at the annual fête in the square, which in those days, before it was repaved, became a sandpit when it rained. Trying to show off a new move, he'd slipped and fell into the mud. Brown streaks covered the brand new trousers he'd bought from Gigot. She laughed and said it looked like he'd shat himself. He laughed as well and they kissed. Six months later they were married.

They'd had good times together especially after Jacques was born. But then after a few years things got stale. Maybe it was the village, the deathly village as everyone left to seek new beginnings. The village where they had grown up and made a small family was now silent.

When Jacques hit eighteen, he left for Paris. At the beginning he returned quite often, but as the years wore on, he visited less. For Jean Marc and Violette that was the end. Once Jacques had gone there seemed no point. Jean Marc refused to leave Crêpe and Violette wanted to leave. They fought and battled and finally Violette gave Jean Marc an ultimatum. Ventrèche or divorce. Jean Marc chose the latter and they split. A year later she married Michel Arnold and Jean Marc disappeared into his thoughts, his TV and his window gazing.

He would have been able to handle it better if Violette had run off with another man. Jean Marc wasn't the greatest husband or lover in the world he accepted that. He was self-centred, self-obsessed, and unambitious. He liked nothing more than tinned duck, ice cream, a cup of tea and a quiet evening in watching game shows. He would have been happy for Violette to find happiness with someone else, a dazzling tycoon from Texas or a dandy Russian in a purple gown. But to move to Ventrèche and marry Michel Arnold was like being kicked in the gut again and again and again until blood spurted out of every hole.

‘Can I smoke here Bernard?’ she asked lighting her fag.

Bernard shrugged. ‘Am I going to stop you?'

'No,' she replied bluntly.

'How’s Jacques by the way?’

‘I don’t know Bernard,’ she said, a tear appearing in her eye.

‘He’s a nice lad. Better than those hooligan two boys Michel had from his first marriage. Criminals they are. Do you see them?’

‘No,’ clarified Violette. ‘They are in prison.’

‘Oh. Good. Best place for them,’ Bernard commented before quickly disappearing into the back.

'I haven't heard from him for ages either,’ said Jean Marc gently once Bernard had made his exit. ‘I try and phone his mobile from time to time - I get free calls you know - but he’s always busy. Paris. Once they go there you lose them forever.'

'You say that every time I see you and each time I think he'll come back to live here in Crêpe, but he never does.'

They sat in silence for a few minutes listening to Bernard cough in the back room. The smell of ancient wine and beer rose up from the floor as the heat of the day increased, bringing with it the ghosts of all the people who had ever drunk at Bar La Boucle.

'So, Violette,' Jean Marc said cautiously. 'What's up?'

She looked round the bar checking to see who was here.

'There's no one here,' Jean Marc confirmed. 'It's only four o'clock, people don't start arriving till sixish.'

'Is that what time this mysterious Glitch starts?'

'Yes - six to half past.'

'Michel told me about it.'

'I'm sure he did.'

'Michel's up to something. I heard something a few nights ago on the phone. Something about he'd pay whatever it takes, but I didn't know who he was talking to.'

'Ah,' scoffed Jean Marc, 'I wouldn't worry about them. Those stupid Gendarmes he's got in his pocket. I've dealt with those clowns.'

'I think it's bigger than that, JM.'

He felt another tug on his memories from forty years ago. He hadn't heard her call him JM for ages. Only Albert called him that on occasions.

'I think he's paying someone. Remember the Gaullist hit squads from the 60s, his father was part of that.'

'I vaguely remember that, but I thought his father was a union man.'

She puffed a cloud of smoke out. 'Ha! Same thing isn't it. Left wing, right wing.' She motioned back and forth with her cigarette leaving a Zorro motif hanging in midair. 'All bloody crooks in my book.'

'Why are you telling me this?'

She took a drag. 'We have a son together. Plus it's my village as well. I was born here and I don't want to see it crushed down again.'

'Why don't you tell your husband that?'

'I don't want you to get hurt.' She was crying now. Sobbing over her glass of Beaujolais. 'I'm sorry, JM, it's all been a bit much. Sometimes I don't know why I left you and the village.'

Jean Marc patted her leg. 'We've been through this before - it's all OK.'

'But this stupid feud between the two villages destroyed a lot of good friendships for the sake of what, a football match?'

'It went back further than that Violette - medieval quarrels and Danish invasions.'

'Oh, who told you that? Madame bloody Coquelicot no doubt. Desperately searching for something interesting to teach the local school kids despite there not being one shred of evidence. It was just mud here in medieval times. Look, my father said everything between the two villages was fine after the war. OK, there was tension, some helped the Germans, some didn't. But that was all forgotten and then your stupid football match happened and everybody fell out again and nothing's been the same since.'

'Look,' said Jean Marc reassuringly. 'Jacques would have left anyway, no matter what would have happened. No young person in their right mind would live here. I mean look at Albert. And Raymond.'

'What about Raymond?' It was Bernard. 'Nothing wrong with Raymond.'

'He's a fine lad,' complimented Jean Marc. 'Just hope he gets to see the world like we never did.'

'What? Go to Paris like Jacques,' Bernard railed. 'And never see him again.'

Violette started sobbed again. 'Will we ever see him again?'

'Of course. We'll invite him to the village fete at the end of August.'

'He won't come,' declared Violette. 'He never comes, he's forgotten us.' She stubbed her fag out in the complimentary bowl of peanuts.

'He'll come back one day. They always do.'

'Do they?

'Yes,' he replied, his voice wavering a touch. 'And if he doesn't,' the Mayor paused, 'I'm sure he'll come back for our funerals.' It could have backfired, she could have stormed out in tears, but the old smile flared up on her face. 'I'm glad you've still got your humour JM.'

'That's what Michel said.'

'Another?' said Bernard coming back out of his room. 'More peanuts?' He looked at the smoking butt in the bowl.

'Sorry,' apologised Violette. 'I shouldn't do that.'

'Don't worry about it, they were from last night anyway. Was just about to chuck them away before you came in.'

'Thanks Bernard,' Violette balked. 'You were always very generous.'

'My pleasure. You want another?'

'Better not. My guts might dissolve. And anyway, I'd better go, that old fart will be back soon from his hunt.' Violette rolled her eyes towards the ceiling and a tiny flake of mascara parachuted off into the air and floated upwards on the spirally updraft from her newly lit cigarette.

'If he's lucky,' Jean Marc added sarcastically. 'If he hasn't been caught in the crossfire. You know what the Gendarmes' marksmanship is like. They're trained on targets fifty feet wide so they don't miss.'

'No they're not, you lie, Jean Marc.'

'It's true. It's what they always say: if you're confronted by a madman waving a gun, don't wait for the gendarmes to shoot him, best do it yourself.'

She giggled that lovely echoing girly squeal. 'Naughty JM.'

'But one final thing.' There was a slight pause. 'Marry Miss Murs, she's always liked you.'

'What! Miss Murs.' Jean Marc tried to look shocked.

'Oh come on Jean Marc, we've all heard the rumours. I have friends here still. Word is you can't stop looking at her.'

'You're all a band of gossip mongers just like your mothers and fathers and grandparents,' cried Jean Marc. 'Don't you people have anything else to talk about apart from who's screwing who, or who isn't screwing anybody, or who's about to screw who, or who's going to die?'

Bernard looked at Violette.

Violette looked at Bernard.

'No. Not really,' he said. 'What else are we meant to talk about?'

Once Violette and her bag of emotions had gone, Jean Marc walked back to the Town Hall and tried to creep up to his apartment. But it was too late, Miss Murs caught him creeping in.

'What did she want?' she asked fiercely. He'd never seen Miss Murs so upright and serious. Normally her neck and head were slightly bent forward carrying her pleasant charm around with her. Now she was as straight as a pin.

'She wanted to warn me about Michel Arnold.'

'Why were you creeping off upstairs to your hidey-hole?"

He hadn't heard the word hidey-hole since he was a child but it fit the description perfectly. 'I need to think Miss Murs.'

'And why couldn't you talk to her here instead of whisking her off to the bar for a drink.'

Jean Marc felt a tinge of anger at this sudden cross-examination by his secretary. 'Miss Murs, she is my ex-wife, who I have a son with, who we never see, and if I want to talk in private, I will. Now if you have something to say regarding the Town Hall or the restaurants, I'm happy to listen, but please don't question me about my ex-wife.'

Miss Murs sagged forward and remained motionless for a few seconds in the Town Hall foyer like she had turned into a hat stand. 'I'm sorry, I just thought. Well, no, it doesn't matter, it's nothing.'

'Go on,' said Jean Marc sympathetically.

'Well, I was just worried. I mean she...'

'She left me and shacked up with that asshole Michel Arnold,' interrupted Jean Marc. 'Is that what you're trying to say.'

'Yes. And I think it was a shoddy thing to do and I don't like her. There I've said it.'

'It's no concern whether you like her or not Miss Murs. To tell you the truth most of the time I don't like her either. But she's the mother of my son and we all have to live with it. But that's not what I wanted to discuss today. This may sound absurd but I wanted to ask you Miss Murs...'

He stopped and stamped his foot. 'I want to ask you.' He stopped again. This was proving more difficult than he imagined and he felt like he was going to have a heart attack.

'I want to ask you Miss Murs,' he said finally. 'If your friend Annette wants to come to dinner one evening to discuss matters regarding Ventrèche. But it doesn't really matter, it can wait until the morning.' And with that he went upstairs and slammed the door.

Chapter 17 - Engaging the Enemy

The next few days were tense. Miss Murs was functional yet terse. The whole thing had turned into a soap opera he wasn't interested in watching any more. A trashy drama complete with an unstable village Mayor, corrupt cops, a neurotic ex-wife, a smouldering romance, a chain of unregistered restaurants and a load of drunken Brits.

One day it might become a film. Those dumb comedies released in the summer holidays in which nothing happens apart from a few short slapstick sketches normally involving people dropping things or crashing into things.

Not that Jean Marc had the remotest idea of what was happening in the world of cinema; the last time he went was in 1980 to see Jaws, which he enjoyed immensely. Partly because he'd never seen a shark - who in rural France had? But mainly because he had never seen the sea either. A feat in itself for a man growing up the latter part of the 20th century. But true all the same.

Which was why the Hawaii trip was so utterly vital to him. This was his Jaws moment. He would kill the shark. He would kill Michel. Kill Ventrèche. Then he would go to Hawaii.

'I'm calling an emergency meeting,' he announced to Miss Murs in the Town Hall foyer. 'Miss Murs, please tell everybody.'

'I'm busy Monsieur Mayor. '

'Miss Murs this is no time for sulking, we have serious business to attend to.'

'What's that?'

'Ventrèche is planning an attack.'

This led to Miss Murs snapping her pencil, with which she was totting up the wages, in half. 'Male overreaction is something I've dealt with for most of my life,' she stammered.

'Yes, but your father was a melodramatic bastard.'

'How dare you talk about my father like that,' she howled.

'It's true!' cried Jean Marc defending his insult. 'Your father and your mother made your life a misery from start to finish, you've even said so yourself. Emotionally blackmailed you into not going to Paris, and then over the course of thirty years ground you down with their wants and whining. The only consolation is that you're here with us now. I may not be the most emotional sort, but you're doing a bloody great job.'

'You're only saying that because you need something. I've been doing this for three months now and you've never said a word of thanks.'

'That's a lie Isabelle, I said it at the beginning of all of this. And I'll say it again. I'm grateful for your effort - truly.'

A bit late in the day thought Miss Murs, and hardly glowing encouragement, but for someone as self centred as Bulot, high praise indeed. 'Well I'll take your word for it Monsieur Mayor,' she said flatly.

'I'm always there to bolster the troops,' he said cheerfully as though he'd saved the lives of millions.

'Just give me a few minutes,' she sighed, 'and I'll gather the troops, as you say. See what war we're fighting today.'

Ten minutes later Miss Murs returned with the rest of the committee/troops: Francis, Bernard, Albert and Ethel in tow. Madame Coquelicot was already there of course, tending to her steaks.

'I don't like leaving my shop unaccounted for Monsieur Mayor,' complained Ethel as soon as she sat down. 'I could lose trade.'

'It's only four o'clock Ethel; there's no one here yet,' Jean Marc calmed her. 'And it's unattended not unaccounted,' he added politely, correcting her French.

'We hear that tramp Violette has been here causing trouble again,' cried out Madame Coquelicot.

'I would prefer, Madame Coquelicot, if my ex-wife and mother of my son was not called a tramp,' he said forcefully, beads of sweat forming on his tanned brow from the searing heat that had descended on the village in recent days. 'Mrs Canet-Bulot-Arnold as she likes to be known these days, came to warn me about a plot by Ventrèche to destroy us.'

Madame Coquelicot burst out laughing, a shred of what looked like steak shot out from her mouth and onto the table where Jean Marc was sitting.

'Thank you Magalie for that,' he said wiping it off with his handkerchief. 'But I've already eaten.'

'Shut up you pompous twerp,' she yelled. 'God, your ex-wife is almost as pretentious as you. Mrs Canet-Bulot-Arnold. What nonsense is that? I remember when you and Violette Canet were little runts of children crying and whining all the time in their poor mothers' arms. If I had my way I would have shot you both.

'You got married and had a son, Jacques, except neither of you had a clue which end your son pissed out of or which end he shat out of. Both as useless as each other, and neither of you have improved much in your adult lives either.'

Jean Marc wiped his forehead. Clearly Madame Coquelicot was in one of her feistier moods.

'Madame Coquelicot,' he started cautiously. 'It's merely a precaution. Violette overheard Michel Arnold that's all. Miss Murs has a friend in Ventrèche as well who has been relaying information to us secretly.'

'So?' wailed Francis standing up. 'We all know people in Ventrèche but I'm not making a great big song and dance about it. In fact, I could tell you what is going on in Ventrèche right now if you want. I could phone my cousin Fabrice if you like.'

'We all know people in Ventrèche Francis thank you, but Annette works in the mayor's office.'

'And? Another cousin Pierre works at the flour mill and I could tell you how they are thinking of poisoning our bread supply.'

'What!'

'It's a joke you dipshit. To point out that perhaps you are all overreacting a bit.'

'Maybe, Francis,' accepted Miss Murs diplomatically. 'But the two hotels are struggling, so is their campsite and Le Vol Au Vent Restaurant, which as you know is part owned by...'

'...Michel Arnold,' Jean Marc finished her sentence off for her. 'Such a stupid name as well.'

'The only thing,' continued Miss Murs, 'that isn't struggling is the castle. But that's because we don't have one.'

'Fact is,' cut in the Mayor. 'We are directly impacting their business, and like all wars they are liable to hit back. Therefore, we need to be careful, that's all I'm saying. Madame Coquelicot. Where do we buy the steaks from?'

'Well, Ventrèche of course, seeing as we don't have a butcher anymore.' She stared at Jean Marc with those old eyes that seemed to shrink back into her hollow head when she was pissed off.

Madame Coquelicot's husband, Cyrille Coquelicot, had been one of the true legends of the village. Not only the village butcher, but a resistance fighter during the war. He'd narrowly escaped disembowelment in the Gestapo guesthouse when the commander had got too drunk that afternoon in the restaurant and decided to go to bed. Four hours later the Americans turned up and shot the commander while he slept, much to the relief of Cyrille who was still hanging upside down from his feet when he was rescued.

After the war, rarely would a night go by without Cyrille regaling the village folk in one of the bars with stories of skewering Germans with sharpened fish slices or deadly filed screwdrivers.

'A day doesn't go past without me thinking of Cyrille, Madame Coquelicot.' Jean Marc boldly announced. 'However, in the interest of public safety for our clients and guests, I'm asking you to change the order and buy the meat from Gigot.'

'Gigot!' she said inhaling deeply into her ancient lungs. 'But that's miles away. Plus, who knows what they do to their meat there, it could be half human.'

'Well it's better than being full of cyanide,' yelled Jean Marc.

'Aren't you being a bit paranoid?' declared Francis.

'They've already blocked the road three times - this week!'

'Yes, you fool,' said Francis. 'But blocking roads is mere school playground antics. Mass poisoning is terrorism. And even Michel Arnold isn't going to go down that route for the sake of his damn restaurant.'

'How do you know?' wailed Jean Marc. 'You didn't play in the football match, did you? You didn't have your leg axed in half by the Quesnoys brothers. You didn't get your face rearranged by a raking elbow from Jean Abat. You didn't see the referee point to the spot when Jacques Breton dived to the ground? And do you know who runs the butchers in Ventrèche now?'

'No.'

'Frederick Lacombe. Scorer of the winning penalty. Same person who supplies our meat. Put two and two together and you've got mass food poisoning.'

Miss Murs slammed her hand on the table. 'Right, that's it. When are we going to stop reminiscing over a football match that took place fifty years ago and start living in the real world?'

'Hear hear,' said Francis and Albert.

'You weren't there Francis Conda.'

'I was in hospital,' exclaimed Francis. 'I had appendicitis.'

'That's not my fault. Maybe if you hadn't been, we might have won the match. Me and you up front, we could have scored a hatful.'

'Jean Marc. Francis. Both of you please sit down.' It was Miss Murs. 'You're making a scene again and I think it's time to move on and forget about this football match once and for all. It's driving me and everyone else here crazy.'

Jean Marc looked like a boy of four, sulking in the corner after someone had stolen his model tractor and tossed it out of the window into the river. But she was right. Even professional footballers and politicians didn't bask in the past as much as he did.

'OK, you're right, Miss Murs. Thank you. I'm just trying my best in difficult circumstances, and I promise not to mention the football match again.'

'Promise,' warned Miss Murs.

'Promise. But I don't trust Michel Arnold, so make sure we're all on guard and remember to watch out for anything suspicious. Secret agents from Ventrèche disguised as tourists, that sort of thing, or hidden cameras recording us pocketing the cash and not giving out receipts. That's the sort of thing these low life clowns in Ventrèche get a thrill out of. Not that there are any petty acts like tax evasion, underage drinking, selling horse steaks disguised as beef, selling diluted wine and turning a blind eye to drink driving. Nothing like that ever happens here in case anybody is listening in.' Jean Marc paused and looked around the room looking for a hidden device disguised as a piano or a shelf.

'This is fun,' declared Madame Coquelicot forgetting her dangerous mood of a few minutes ago. 'It's like the war again.'

'Well,' commented Francis. 'I think you are all getting a bit paranoid.

'I bet that's what they said before Pearl Harbour. Then look what happened.'

'Slightly different scenario,' muttered Francis. 'But I'll let you have your fun.'

'And fun I will,' exclaimed Jean Marc seen looking decidedly unhinged.

'Can we go now? It was Albert getting to his feet.

'Yep, beer time,' declared Francis also getting up.

'But just one minute please,' Jean Marc cried out, mightily relieved to have got around to the real reason he had called the meeting.

'I've one last announcement. A very important thing before you go. Thank you. Yes. Ermm. Excuse me. Err. Miss Murs will you marry me.'

It came out a lot easier than he had practiced in front of the mirror a hundred times that morning. Unfortunately, no one was listening. Not even Miss Murs who was busy putting files into her bag.

'Thank you,' he said again knowing if he didn't seize the moment now it would be lost forever. 'Excuse me did anybody hear me?'

'What was that?' asked Miss Murs gathering up her bag and preparing to leave. 'Marriage announcements? You said not to bother with the notices anymore.' And resumed getting ready to go out with the rest.

'Miss Murs,' whined Jean Marc getting exasperated with the situation. 'I'm not sure you heard me correctly.'

'Say again,' she said.

'Oh God!' he cried out and walked over to her, bent down on his knees, his back creaking like a basket, and asked her again. Loudly this time.

'Miss Murs, will you marry me?'

Miss Murs spun round her eyes transfixed on the ring Jean Marc had produced from his jacket pocket. It was his grandmother's, who had been born in Gigot and 'emigrated' to Crêpe for reasons no one in living memory could fathom. Gigot wasn't Paris, it wasn't even Rennes or Dijon or Pau or any other half interesting provincial town in the country. It was conservative, stuffy and inconsequential. But compared to Crêpe (or Ventrèche) especially a hundred years ago, it was heaven.

'Oh God, it's beautiful, Jean Marc. Where did you get it?'

'Err,' he stalled. 'From Hausens in Gigot - top of the range.'

'It's so sparkly.'

Jean Marc felt like he was kneeling on nails, the tree knots in the uneven floorboards digging into his knees and he was wondering how long he would have to stay like this waiting for the answer. Or was Miss Murs going to admire the ring for the next twenty years. Or perhaps she had misread the situation completely and thought it was simply a present.

‘What stones are they Jean Marc, ruby?’

‘I think so.’

The rest of the committee were simply frozen. Puppets left dangling on their hooks after the puppeteer had gone home.

'So?' cried the Mayor.

‘Oh,’ she cried. ‘Yes, sorry.’ Her eyes welling up. ‘I mean, yes, I will marry you.’

Jean Marc silently sighed and got to his feet again and kissed her.

‘I thought you’d never ask,’ she said when they’d finished. ‘I’ve been waiting twenty years for this.’

‘Try it on.’

Miss Murs took the ring and jammed it onto her finger; it fitted perfectly. Fate, Jean Marc supposed. He had given the same ring to Violette, but it hadn’t fit, so he had to buy a new one that cost him about two months wages.

‘Have you finished?’ cried Madame Coquelicot dropping back down from her hook. ‘Thought I was going die waiting for you two.'

‘Me too,’ chipped Francis. ‘But congratulations anyway. Well done, bloody took you long enough.’ He gave a short handclap but no one joined in.

‘Can we go now?’ asked Albert totally impervious to the romantic situation unfolding before him.

'Yes, you can all go now,' declared Jean Marc visibly relieved. 'But keep the day of the Summer Fete open. The wedding day will be on the same day - 1st September.’

‘Do we have to work that day?' asked Albert.

'Of course you have to work, Albert. It'll be the busiest day of the year. We can call it Crêpe Day.'

‘Bloody Crêpe,’ Albert moaned. ‘Should have left the place years ago.’

‘You can after this,’ smiled Jean Marc.

‘Where would I go?’ asked Albert who actually seemed to be seriously considering going on holiday for the first time ever.

‘Anywhere you want Albert?’ beamed Miss Murs. ‘Paradise if you want?’

‘Paradise,’ he repeated his eyes gazing over in wonder. ‘But where’s that?’

‘Hawaii,’ blurted out Jean Marc. Then checked himself. ‘But not the first two weeks of October, that's when we’re going and the last thing in the world I want is sharing my dream holiday with you Albert. No offence.'

Albert shrugged. 'I can't say I would want to spend my holiday with you either.' And wandered off.

‘Did you say, we?’ asked Miss Murs, her face lit up like a thousand cake candles.

‘Yes,’ exclaimed Jean Marc. ‘We are both going to Hawaii, and nothing, not even Michel Arnold and his armies of darkness will stop us!'

Chapter 18 - Chris Waddle

'Great day for a wedding,' remarked Ethel Budd looking up into the clear blue September sky as she opened her shop.

'A perfect day,' Jean Marc replied in English walking past her shop on his morning walk to survey the village on what was possibly the most important day since 1967. That huge event in his life he wasn't allowed to speak about any more.

'Pissing down in England my nephew says,' Ethel continued in English. She spoke French most of the time, but some mornings, as she freely admitted, she simply couldn't be bothered.

'Will he be over next week as normal?' asked the Mayor.

'Aye. Although the last trip he did last week was met by a few suspicious heads at customs. Bringing over all those cases of brown ale down for the big day.'

'The big day?'

'The wedding. It's what we say back home when someone gets married.'

'Ah,' realised Jean Marc. 'Of course. *Le Grand Jour.*'

Jean Marc had often thought he would like to live in England. Maybe Newcastle where Ethel's nephew still lived. Jean Marc supported Marseille. Not because it was particularly near - about 500 kms near in fact - but because Chris Waddle used to play for them in the early nineties. The epitome of the English footballer abroad. Spoke almost no French and from his accent almost no English. But people loved him. Half walking half running round the field with his flat top mullet and charming boyish looks. He was never going to be Pele, Maradona or Messi. He wasn't even next to Cruyff, Platini or Zidane, but you felt something could happen when he got the ball. One of those Hollywood crossfield passes that could dissect a defence like a scalpel. Or a mazy run through a line of rugged defenders from Corsica. And then there were those games when he did absolutely nothing. Hang about near the touchline with his shirt hanging out thinking of a pint or two after the game. Then he left and went back to England. Sheffield Wednesday maybe? Sheffield Mercredi - strange name. And yet twenty-five years later whenever people talk about Marseille, Magic Chris pops up as though he was still donning the famous blue in the Stade Velodrome.

'Are you nervous?' she asked.

Jean Marc picked up a can of baked beans from the shelf and tossed it into the air so it spun in the air a few times, then caught it again. The French did a version called *Haricot Blancs à la Tomate* but it wasn't the same. Too firm and bitter. The beans rattling around in your stomach like small pieces of Lego. The sauce watery and chalky.

'No. Not in the slightest. I've done it before.'

'I thought of getting married once,' said Ethel Budd putting her newsstand outside with her selection of English newspapers three days out of date. 'But the one man I liked, loved even, was a doctor, who was happily married to another doctor. So I decided if I couldn't have him, I might as well not bother. It's quite a Victorian ideal I know, but I don't regret it at all. As I've told you plenty of times Jean Marc, I've had a very happy life.'

‘And long may the good times continue,’ Jean Marc announced rather formally. What would the village do without Miss Budd he thought as he watched her fuss over the newsstand that had once belonged to the grocer to display packets of figs on.

‘How’s Jacques by the way, is he coming?’

‘No.’ Jean Marc wasn’t sure what else to say.

‘That’s a shame; I haven’t seen him for years.’

‘Neither have I.’

‘Still moving pianos?’

‘Yes.’

Jacques worked for a piano seller moving pianos from one rich fucker's house to another rich fucker's house when the slightly wealthier rich fucker bought a more expensive one and sold the old one to the slightly poorer rich fucker.

That’s how his son had explained it to Francis one evening on a rare visit to Crêpe while they were both blasted on strong Ventoux.

His son had done it for years. Before that he worked in bars and restaurants cheffing, waitering, drinking, partying. He would have loved to visit his son - he had a nice flat in the 13th, but each time a visit had been mentioned Jacques had fobbed him off with an excuse.

Jean Marc knew he lived with a man and had done for years. Jean Marc couldn’t give a toss - half the Italian miners were as bent as the nails they used to hammer into the wooden supports in the dark mines. But Violette minded. Which is why she never visited, even though she missed him dearly.

Jean Marc made a mental note to visit Jacques with Miss Murs whether his son liked it or not. They would just turn up - surprise surprise. Remember my secretary, she’s now your new mum, this must be François your lover. Bonjour! I’m your father-in-law...Let's go to dinner! I'm buying. Have you ever been to Hawaii...'

It probably wouldn't be that easy, but after all of this, maybe it would.

'What time will the festivities start by the way?' asked Ethel Budd now unpacking a carton of Fray Bentos pies. Another English culinary oddity. An upside-down pie filled with dog food. Of course, he didn't tell her that: he said it was lovely. 'So fresh!'

'The usual time,' announced Jean Marc. 'Let's see. We plan to get married at fiveish, then have a meal say at six-thirty. Once that's over, we can get drunk and dance to Ray Gun.'

'Of yes, I love Raymond's music - so modern and funky.'

'Yes. It is funky.'

'Best part of the year for me. I'll be there,' said Ethel. 'But don't be late for your wedding, I know what happened last time?'

'I wish people would stop telling me that. It wasn't my fault.'

'Men always have an excuse, I think it's why I never bothered.'

Chapter 19 - Tourist Trader

'Have you seen this?' his soon-to-be-wife exclaimed excitedly as Jean Marc wandered back into La Crêperie a few minutes after saying goodbye to Ethel Budd. 'Someone's left a review of La Crêperie on Tourist Trader.'

Jean Marc's mind drifted back to that first afternoon of Le Glitch. He would never forget them. Alex Cassidy, his wife Sandra and their red-faced son, Tim. The boy mocking him because Crêpe didn't have a listing.

Not any more squirt. Not now Miss Murs had whipped up Crêpe's very own Tourist Trader listing entitled:

Visit the Revolutionary Hooks of Crêpe.

Legend had it that during the French Revolution, the Marquise of Gigot and his court were strung up from the beams in the committee room by brass hooks. Hooks which were still there as bright and as polished as the day they were screwed in, owing to Albert's secret formula of caustic soda and Bernard's red wine. A solution that could probably bring out the Eiffel Tower in a silver glint if enough was applied. It worked a treat and as the guests ate their steak-frites they could look up and wonder what it would be like to be hung up from various parts of their body by brass hooks.

Other must-see attractions included the 16th century classic French square - *Place de Crêpe* (recently relaid). An 18th century neoclassical church. An early 19th century bronze sculpture of Jeanne d'Arc on horseback, and a post-industrial guided nature trail along the colliery's old slag heaps accompanied by a real-life ex-miner, Francis Conda.

Until this review Miss Murs was now reading, all four attractions had attracted zero views, likes or comments. Which had prompted Albert to suggest there were remote Andean outposts with more social media interactions than Crêpe.

'How many stars did it get?' asked Jean Marc eagerly.

'You read it,' she said passing Jean Marc her iZen tablet.

Restaurant Name: La Crêperie de Crêpe

Food: Crêpes

Location: Crêpe

Country: France

Reviews: 1/1

Reviewer said: *After a long journey through the dark lanes of rural France, my husband and I were most delighted to stumble upon lovely eatery nestled in the heart of the village of Crêpe.*

'Bloody hell,' the Mayor commented. 'It's like reading *La Gloire de Mon Pere* by Marcel Pagnol.'

'Just continue reading,' she insisted.

We were greeted by the lovely owner Isabelle and were treated to a feast of fresh pancakes as soft and as light as clouds. Inside was a rich fondant of cream, chocolate, orange rind and honey. A mesmeric delight for the senses and something my husband Jeff said he'd never experienced before. An absolute find. Classic France Classic Crêpes! 5/5

‘Five out of five stars!’ Jean Marc nearly jumped out of his seat, almost tossing the tablet through the window of the restaurant. 'Wait till Michel Asshole Arnold sees this.'

'Jean Marc,' screamed Miss Murs. 'For the last time, this isn't about Ventrèche, this is about us and Crêpe.'

'Agreed Isabelle. This is about us. But God those Brits are so gullible, aren't they? I mean it’s only a bloody pancake, hardly a culinary masterpiece.'

‘It’s the way I sprinkle sugar on them,’ she said sarcastically reining in a huge desire to smash a pan over the Mayor’s head and cancel the whole stupid marriage.

‘You’re a genius Miss Murs. Well done!’ The Mayor gave her a kiss, totally oblivious to his high-minded chauvinist ideals.

‘Please, Jean Marc, call me Isabelle,’ she said. ‘We are getting married in a few hours.’

‘Yes. Of course. In fact, should we even be seeing each other,’ he said backing away slightly. ‘Isn’t it bad luck? Aren’t you meant to have a day off before you commit?’

‘You make it sound like we’re going to prison.’

‘Hawaii isn’t prison, Isabelle,’ he said keenly reminding her that last week he'd put down a deposit on a fancy resort for both of them. ‘In a month’s time we’ll be away on a hot golden beach.’

'What happens when we go away. What happens if people visit and we get a bad review: "Classic France! Closed!" There was an audible sense of panic in her voice.

‘We can put a sign up. Closed for two weeks and reopen it after we get back. Who’s going to come here in winter anyway?’

Miss Murs looked at her husband-to-be-in-three-hours. ‘But Le Glitch, it’s not going to shut up for winter is it? People will still come even if they weren’t planning to - just like now.’

That stunned the Mayor. For the entire summer the Mayor had assumed the Glitch would simply stop when he did. A throwback perhaps to his old life as a postman when he assumed that when he was on holiday everyone else was.

'Good heavens!' he exclaimed. 'You're right Miss Murs. Isabelle. Why would it stop?'

'Which brings me to another problem. We promised Albert and Francis the winter off. Who's going to man the pumps?'

'Well it's their choice. They can still work if they want to. If not, we can employ other people. There are a lot of young people looking for a job these days. Gigot has 20% unemployment. People might decide this is the place to be. Crêpe - centre of the universe! Jacques might even come back.'

Miss Murs gave her fiancé a kiss. 'That would be nice wouldn't it. Old Jacky back where he belongs,' she declared hopefully. 'He's got plenty of experience of the restaurant trade, hasn't he?'

'Exactly! The dynasty isn't dead yet Miss Murs,' he said. 'Look, I'm going for a few jars with Francis and Bernard down Bar La Boucle. I'll see you later.'

'Well don't be late. Francis told me about your last wedding.'

'That wasn't my fault. It was the British Royal Family's.'

This bit was half true. On his first wedding day Violette had insisted on getting married early because their wedding day coincided with the date of the Royal Wedding between Lady Di and Prince Charles. The night before he had got drunk with Francis and so missed the start of his wedding which was at ten o'clock sharp. He spent his entire afternoon nursing his hangover watching the Royal Wedding in Violette's mother's lounge with a load of her friends saying

'Doesn't she look nice,' over and over again for the whole damn ceremony that seemed to last years.

'I won't be late, promise, I'll be over at the Town Hall at five p.m. sharp. We should have it all wrapped up by six then we can eat and listen to Ray Gun.' And sauntered off smiling downstairs to Bar La Boucle.

As a young girl Miss Murs had dreamt of her wedding day. The flowers, the crowds, the cheering. And yet now it was finally upon her after so many years, it was all going to be wrapped up in half an hour with a handful of people in attendance. She wasn't resentful though, she loved the Crêperie and what they were doing, plus she was happy beyond belief to be getting married to this man she had loved and loathed for so many years.

Chapter 20 - Kevin Arthur

‘Are you going to ring the church bells for your wedding?’ Bernard remarked sitting outside Bar La Boucle.

‘Nah,’ said Jean Marc. ‘I like the silence.’

‘Too right,’ said Francis. ‘Can’t believe we didn’t turn them off sooner.’

‘Like when we were born,’ added Bernard. ‘Then we wouldn’t have had to get up to go to school.’

‘Madame Coquelicot would have found you Bernard,’ Jean Marc reminded him.

Bernard looked terrified. ‘God. When she was angry, she was angry.’

'Still is,' concurred the Mayor making a face.

They all laughed and chinned their glasses. They'd had their battles over the years. They had fought and hadn’t spoken for weeks. But there was a bond of understanding even if the understanding was sometimes lost in Francis’ alcoholism, Jean Marc’s idleness, or Bernard’s moroseness. Now perhaps in their twilight years, they could look forward to happy times ahead.

‘Another for the road?' suggested Francis proffering his glass.

'Why not,' said Jean Marc looking up the road towards the bypass.

Bernard brought the drinks out a few minutes later. ‘Dead today isn't it?' he remarked.

‘Just what I was thinking,’ said Jean Marc.

‘Maybe we should turn those bells on after all,’ quipped Francis. 'Make some noise.'

'Mmm,' murmured Jean Marc, a chilly wind blew through him as though winter had stepped in through the door. ‘Something doesn’t feel right.’ He glanced at his watch nervously.

‘It’s only four-thirty,' Francis reminded him. 'What's the problem? The Glitch doesn't turn itself on till six at least.'

‘Mmm,’ Jean Marc mmm-ed again. ‘That’s true, but it feels so eerie this evening. As though the ghosts of the past have risen up with the express purpose of ruining my big day.’

Francis took a pull on his drink. ‘The only ghosts here are me, you and Bernard.’

‘All those old people we used to laugh at and goad for dancing the waltz. Throwing water bombs from the church tower. Or spitting on them. Feeling Madame Lafarge's breasts while pretending to peck her on the cheek and wish her Bonne Fête. All the people we've double-crossed, back stabbed, and insulted. All coming back to get us when things are going right. It wouldn't surprise me, knowing this village.

‘Get a grip of yourself Jean Marc, you’re getting married today and it will be a ball. I bet we’ll have to get Albert to barricade the entrance to the village there will be so many people coming to the wedding.’

‘I’ll have another one, Bernard,’ ordered Jean Marc necking his drink. ‘A double in fact.’

‘A double?’ A stunned Francis said remembering Jean Marc weakness for alcohol.

‘Yes, a double,’ the Mayor declared. ‘You don’t get married every day, do you? Jump to it Bernard.’

But in truth his thoughts weren’t with the merits of the sour apply liqueur called Pineau. Or the fact that he was getting married. His thoughts had moved onto the more serious matter of the €1000 deposit he'd put down on their dream Hawaiian holiday. The remaining balance to be paid on 31st September, the day before they were planning to fly out.

'Please God,' he prayed silently looking up at the church tower. ‘Not now. Don’t stop the Glitch. I need that money. Just another month then you can do whatever you want. Burn the place down for all I care.’

‘Le Glitch has probably gone back to normal,' joked Bernard as he brought Jean Marc his double Pineau. ‘Or someone's turned it off.'

'Do you think it's possible?' asked Jean Marc, panic rising.

'My grandson’s friend Kevin from Ventrèche seems to think so, he's a bit of a technical wizard or something, says one day it'll go back to how it was.’

‘What!!!!' Jean Marc exploded, hardly believing what he was hearing. ‘Why didn’t you mention this before?’

‘You never asked,’ said Bernard. ‘Plus I haven’t got a clue about this sort of stuff. Ask Raymond, he'll know.'

'Raymond!' Bernard shouted towards his house five doors away. Moments later a pale goofy teenager stuck his huge head out of the window.

‘Yeh.’

It was hard to believe that this teenager (the only son of Bernard's daughter’s doomed marriage to a psychotic policeman in Dijon, who had chosen to live in Crêpe with his grandfather instead of with his nutcase parents) had been doing the village disco for so many years, despite the fact he was still only sixteen.

'Come out here,' ordered Jean Marc in a dictatorial manner.

'Why?' Raymond shouted.

'Our Mayor would like to see you,' said Bernard.

'Why now?' moaned the kid.

'Because I'm getting married in a minute,' shouted Jean Marc.

Three minutes later the lanky youth sidled up wearing a brown hoodie as thick as a sheepskin coat and a baseball cap with a peak the size of an aeroplane wing. 'What's up?' he said in a sort of Parisian gangster patois.

'Sit down and tell us about your friend Kevin,' ordered Jean Marc.

Raymond fell into a seat in his grandfather's bar like he was getting into bed. A bored expression spread across his spotty face. 'Kevin who?' Raymond answered, rubbing his thin papery beard.

Jean Marc eyeballed the kid. 'Don't get smart, Raymond. How many Kevins are there at your school?'

'Err, four,' countered Raymond smugly looking at his granddad to signal he'd got one over this old giffer. 'Kevin Boise, Kevin Vincent...'

'Yes yes yes,' growled the Mayor. 'But who is this tech wizard?' He pronounced tech wizard like an exotic fruit.

'Tech wizard?' Raymond hesitated, 'Who's the tech wizard?'

'The one who was talking about Le Glitch!' Jean Marc was about to blow his top.

'Kevin Arthur you mean.'

'Kevin Arthur?' Jean Marc looked puzzled. 'Doesn't sound very French?'

'It's not. He's English,' Raymond said blankly. 'Well his parents are. Or one is, I'm not sure. But he was born here, speaks French.'

'What does he do?'

Ray looked at his grandfather again then back at the Mayor. 'He doesn't do anything, he's a school kid.'

'I know that Raymond,' Jean Marc blazed, reaching for his drink. 'I mean what does he do in his spare time?'

'I don't know.'

'I thought you said he was a friend?'

'I said he was in my year.'

'What did he say about Le Glitch then?'

'Nothing really. He just said it'd go back to normal one day, I only heard him say it in the dinner queue. I wasn't even speaking to him. He was speaking to someone else. Why? What's the problem?'

'Why don't you look up the street,' suggested Jean Marc pointing. 'What do you see?'

The boy squinted and pulled the Concorde-sized peak of his cap down to protect him from the sun. 'Err, what am I meant to be looking at? I can't see anything.'

'That's exactly my point,' confirmed Jean Marc. 'There is no one.'

Raymond looked at his watch. 'But it's only four forty. The Glitch doesn't activate itself until half past six. Or six thirty-two, if you want to be precise.' He looked at his watch again.

'How do you know that?' demanded the Mayor.

'Because I sit at my window like you do. I record things, monitor things, analyse data, I mean, what else am I meant to do here.'

'You chose to live here,' Jean Marc reminded him.

'I chose not to live with my parents. I did not choose to live in Crêpe. There's a difference.'

The three men accepted the point like three wise men who'd known the impending destruction of planet Earth but didn't tell anyone.

'Well hang on,' cried Raymond. 'There is someone.'

'Who?' Jean Marc exclaimed jumping out of his seat.

'It looks like Miss Murs standing by the Town Hall, she looks all dressed up.'

'Shit! I'll speak to you later. Stay put. Unless you're coming to my wedding.'

The boy laughed.

'OK, well, stay put,' accepted the Mayor. 'Francis, finish your drink. You're marrying me remember. I mean us.' He pointed to Miss Murs who was now looking across angrily to them all.

'Do I have to?' moaned Francis. 'I'm just settling into a nice drinking rhythm.'

'Yes.'

'Can't Albert do it?'

'No. You're the best man, plus Albert would ask too many questions and he might drop the rings.'

'What do I have to do?

'Nothing. Read from the manual. It's easy, any idiot could do it.'

'Why didn't you ask the priest?'

'I did. Said he was busy.'

Chapter 21 - The Young Couple

The wedding passed off as uneventfully as any register marriage could in a deserted backwater of France. Miss Isabelle Marie Murs and Jean Marc Alain Bulot were wed in ten minutes flat by a drunk deputy Mayor in front of four people: A baby-faced maintenance man wearing a Def Leppard T-shirt; a retired English nurse in a spotted house dress; an old baker wearing an Olympique Marseille tracksuit; and a ninety-two year old ex school teacher wearing all black. You couldn't have made it up and no one tried.

The only record of the event apart from an illegibly filled in marriage certificate were the photos Albert took on his 1980s Kodak Click-o-Matic camera. Unable to develop it anywhere on planet earth he secretly hoped aliens might one day find it, and using their advanced technology develop the film and add it to their understanding of human life: Five badly dressed villagers attending a wedding in a village hall disguised as a Texan steakhouse. The total product of two million years of human evolution.

Not that any of this was bothering Jean Marc. His only concern, as he walked out on his wedding day, was why there was no one in the village. He hated Westerns but he felt he was starring in one. Trapped in a town with John Wayne, Clint Eastwood and Lee van Cleff. Plus Jean Marc Bulot, the only Frenchman, stalked by assassins, murderers and Mexican bandits.

'Everybody follow me,' he suddenly ordered pointing towards the bypass.

'I'm sorry?' cried a startled Miss Murs.

'To the bypass,' he roared.

'Why!' she howled already cursing married life and she'd only been at it for five minutes. 'Have you lost your mind or something?'

'Yes,' he agreed. 'But just follow me anyway.'

Thirty minutes later Jean Marc, Miss Murs, Francis, Albert and Bernard were standing on the bypass like leftovers from a circus after trudging down and up the hill to the bypass in their wedding garb.

'Why are we here?' Bernard complained trying to be heard against the roaring traffic.

'I'm looking for a British license plate. If you see one flag it down.'

'Flag it down?' repeated Francis.

'Just do it. I'm taking charge, this is a very serious situation, and you must do what I say. For once.'

'There, there! An old orange VW camper,' Miss Murs cried pointing down the road.

'Where?' said Jean Marc.

'That great orange blob, you blind git,' she yelled pointing to the brightly coloured vehicle, behind it a mass of cars trying to get past. 'I thought you were a car expert?'

'I am, I just haven't got my glasses on. Oh yes, I see it now. Flag it down.'

'But why?' moaned Francis.

'I'll explain later. Try to look injured or something.'

Francis doubled over clutching his belly while Miss Murs and Albert jumped up and down like loonies trying to catch the attention of the vehicle. The camper saw them and desperate to get away from the honking traffic behind, pulled off the bypass and onto the road to Crêpe.

'Bonjour,' greeted Jean Marc as the sliding door of the camper opened and a man with slicked back jet black hair wearing brown moleskin trousers and a checked shirt open to the navel, and who bore a mild resemblance to F. Scott Fitzgerald, stepped out and shook the Mayor's hand firmly.

'Bonjour,' he said. 'Is he injured or something?' he said in flawless French.

'He looks in a bad state,' said the girl, a waif like twentysomething dressed in a pink rose patterned dress.

'Oh him, he's fine,' said Jean Marc. 'Stomach cramp.'

'Are you lost or something?' the Young Man asked looking at the ensemble.

'We're on the way to a wedding,' stated Miss Murs.

'In Crêpe,' clarified Jean Marc.

'Oh my,' cried the girl. 'That's where we're going. Apparently, they do the best Crêpes in France - we read it on Tourist Trader.'

Miss Murs' face lit up like the million birthday cake candles she'd never had as a child because her parents were too miserly. 'Oh my God,' she exclaimed. 'That's us, we run the Crêperie.'

'Whoopee,' the girl cried.

'What a coincidence,' agreed the Young Man. 'Because we were having trouble finding you.' He picked up a tattered copy of a 2011 French Road Atlas. 'Couldn't find you anywhere.'

'Give me that here,' demanded the Mayor tutting and grabbing the atlas. 'Ah, IGN,' he exclaimed looking at the cover of the Atlas. 'The world's greatest map makers. Of course, it's on here.'

'Still couldn't find it?' insisted the Young Man smugly.

'You're probably looking in the wrong place,' rebuked the Mayor. 'There's another Crêpe in Aude. Except that one is spelt differently - it doesn't have a circumflex.'

'Oh, we found that one,' declared the girl.

'IGN mapped half of Africa in the 18th century,' continued the Mayor. 'I'm sure they managed to include Crêpe - it would be like missing off Paris or Rome or London.'

But it wasn't. Even the official French state cartographers had failed to include Crêpe. Gigot was there, Ventrèche was there, even Plante was there. Even Crepe in Aude was there. But not Crêpe in Gigot County. In the middle of the triangle between Ventreche, Plante and Gigot, where Crêpe should have been, was an empty blank white space.

'What scale is this?' demanded the Mayor impatiently.

'1:1.25.'

'Too small.'

'It's the biggest they do,' countered the Young Man.

'Anyway,' cut in the Young Girl realising the poor man was about to blow a fuse. 'We fired up the old satnav instead. But weirdly Crêpe didn't show up on that either. As though it had been wiped off the face of the planet.'

'Thanks, you don't have to rub it in,' scolded the Mayor. 'We did have a functioning coal mine once. And a post office, three bars, a police station and a hairdresser.'

'Sorry,' she apologised.

'So anyway, we tried again,' continued the Young Man. 'But no luck. Every time we punched in Crêpe nothing happened.'

'You must be wrong,' said Francis. 'I worked down the mine.'

'Of course they're wrong,' added Miss Murs. 'Crêpe is one of the 36,000 official communes in France.'

'It's probably a Glitch then,' offered the Young Man innocently.

'You know about Le Glitch?' the Mayor asked.

'The what?'.

'Le Glitch!' cried Jean Marc. 'It's the key to everything. It's why we are here on this bypass.'

Now the Young Couple really looked confused.

'You got anything to drink in there?' Francis asked the Young Man, not feeling any need to stand on ceremony at this crucial juncture in their lives.

'Wine,' replied the girl. 'It's uncorked though, it might have soured a touch. And it is from the supermarket.'

Francis flapped his arms in the air signalling he'd drink petrol if there was nothing else available as he grabbed the bottle from the girl and refilled his belly with a huge slug of the half-opened bottle of Bergerac. 'Lovely drop,' he congratulated as the liquid drained from his stomach into his vein-streaked face via a series of arteries and capillaries that in their lifetime had transported more red wine than a 19th century Bordeaux-Bristol bound steamer.

'Don't finish it,' ordered Jean Marc snatching it from his friend and taking a deep pull.

'Maybe you should explain what's been going on?' said the girl gently.

Chapter 22 - The Book

After Jean Marc's long and short history of Crêpe, the wine gone and another bottle opened plus a bag of peanuts, the Mayor finally finished his rambling story.

‘Let me get this straight,’ summed up the Young Man. ‘Before Le Glitch, no one ever visited the village. Then came Le Glitch and people.'

'Yes,' nodded the Mayor. 'Everyone who was originally going to Ventrèche along the bypass was diverted to Crêpe. Initially I thought the visitors had switched their satnavs to SCENIC MODE sending them along the old road which before the bypass took people from Gigot to Ventrèche via Crêpe and Plante.'

'Is there such a thing as a SCENIC MODE,' asked the Young Man looking baffled.

‘I'm not sure,' said the Mayor. 'Probably not. But the point I was making at the time was that just because we have all this technology, doesn’t mean people know how to use it. They just switch it on and away they go. They could be driving to the end of the world for all they care. Instead they ended up in Crêpe. Which I suppose is the same thing...'

The Young Man was impressed with the Mayor's logic. 'But they didn't end up in Crêpe, did they?' enthused the Young Man. 'At least they thought they didn't. Because when they arrived, they thought they were in Ventrèche because there was no sign.'

'Yes, that is true.' Jean Marc looked at Albert. 'A responsibility that lies solely at the feet of our maintenance man here.'

The Young Man defended Albert. 'No, but don't you see. By having no sign it fooled them into thinking they were in Ventrèche. In many ways all of your success is down to Albert.'

Albert beamed a full lollipop smile to everyone.

'Well I wouldn't go that far,' complained the Mayor. 'I mean all the planning was all down to me. I facilitated Le Glitch as it were.'

'So you were all involved. That's great!' applauded the Young Man desperately trying to avoid a bust up among these people who looked totally exhausted. 'But getting back to the present. Now *Le Glitch* has turned itself off and the village is dead again? Yes?'

Everyone nodded.

'What are you going to do?' asked the Young Girl.

'Interrogate a turd of a boy called Raymond,' commanded Jean Marc

'Who's Raymond?' asked the Young Girl feverishly excited.

'A traitor. He's Bernard Cle's grandson. You'll meet him in a minute. Are you hungry?'

The Young Couple looked at each other. 'Actually,' said the Young Man, 'we're bloody starving. Those peanuts were all we had.'

'It's your lucky day then,' said Jean Marc pointing to the road leading to the village. 'Can you give us a lift?'

'Of course,' agreed the Young Man. 'Get in. This is all fascinating stuff,' he declared. 'You see I was wondering whether you minded if I wrote this down? I'm writing a book you see.'

Jean Marc slapped his forehead hard with his hand as though he was swatting a gigantic fly. This was slowly becoming the worst day of his life. 'Not another one,' he yelled. 'I can't believe it, another Englishman writing a book on France. I mean, what is there to write about?'

'Oh come on,' the Young Man objected. 'Nice weather, good wine, great markets. What more could people want?'

Jean Marc answered abruptly. 'You're just the same as Henry Clark and the rest of them.'

'Who's Henry Clark?'

'Another prat looking for the real France - restaurants, brocantes, markets. I mean who cares about the real France. This is the real France and it's shit!' The Mayor gestured to his village folk and the empty deserted fields. 'Trust me, I've lived here all my life! I know.'

'But I'm not doing just another book on France,' he insisted. 'This is different.'

Jean Marc nearly choked. 'That's what they all say.'

'I'm looking for stories, real stories about real people,' argued the Young Man. 'A book on real France - an offbeat guidebook to France you never thought existed.'

'Oh God,' moaned the Mayor. 'I mean Napoleon would love this, wouldn't he? All you Englishmen gushing about France as though Waterloo had never happened.'

'This is all so frustrating.' The Young Man rubbed his face like he was trying to pull it off. 'I hate these people like this Henry Clarkson or whatever you called him. All these semi-retired drunks driving around in Range Rovers wearing panama hats and carrying brown satchel bags and indestructible Samsonite cases full of heavy trousers and thick soled shoes. Whose wives wear badly fitting hats and blow torch you with bad breath every time they open their cavernous mouths. Not to mention the stupid banana-faced dogs in the back seat called Rutland, Wensleydale or Sniper.'

'Or Leicester,' joined in Jean Marc remembering the Terry Towelled mutt in the back of Henry Clark's car.

'Yesss,' cried the Young Man in agreement. 'There's millions of these old farts trudging round France in their 4x4s writing books full of yawningly boring reviews of crap restaurants serving tripe and horse meat. In which every other word is RUSTIC or FARMHOUSE and every photo is of a bottle of wine, a cracked peppercorn or a piece of bread. All from stock photos off the internet because when they got home, they'd realised they had got their iPhones the wrong way round and were in fact taking pictures of themselves.'

'Have you finished?' said Francis looking like he was about to kill the Young Man if he didn't stop squealing soon.

'Yes,' the Young Man said solemnly.

'I have a question though,' asked the Young Girl.

'One last question,' Francis informed her.

'Who's wedding is it?'

'Ours,' said the Mayor smiling. 'And my wife. Miss Murs.'

'Yes,' said Miss Murs. 'We got married about an hour ago. I know it's weird but this is what we do in France all the time, stand around on roadsides after our dream wedding.'

'Oh. Congratulations,' the Young Girl said intuitively hugging the bride.

'Yes. Congratulations,' the Young Man offered his hand in true English fashion.

Chapter 23 - Raymond Clé

After piling into the young couple's camper and driving the two kilometres to Crêpe, they were now all sitting on the tables outside the Town Hall waiting for their Crêpes which Annette from Ventrèche had kindly prepared. (Miss Murs, on virtue of the fact that it was her wedding day, had given herself the day off.)

'Who is this mysterious Raymond then?' asked the Young Man tucking into a Crêpe Suzette, a rather sweet and sickly affair favoured by the sweet-toothed English.

'That lanky fool over there setting up the DJ equipment,' Jean Marc said pointing to the village square.

'Watch it Bulot!' butted in Bernard. 'That's my grandson you're talking about. Just leave Raymond out of this, he's got nothing to do with it, he's just a kid.'

'He's hiding something and I know it.'

'I doubt it Jean Marc. He's just a kid who hates his parents and spends most of his time reading or listening to music. He wouldn't hurt a fly.'

'The silent type,' mused Jean Marc.

'Look,' implored Bernard. 'Whatever you do, don't cancel the event. He looks forward to this all year. It'll crush him if it's cancelled and he'll moan about it for months and I have to live with him.'

'Well it depends on him, doesn't it?'

‘Just be gentle,’ pleaded the old baker.

‘Raymond!' Jean Marc bellowed across the square. 'Here. Hurry up, we haven’t got all day - get over here.’

‘Yes Monsieur,' the kid said when he finally walked over to the bank of tables.

‘You hungry?

‘Not really,’ he shrugged. ‘A bit.’

'Well sit down and have a Crêpe and tell me everything you know about Kevin Arthur.’

'I’ve told you. I don't really know him,' moaned Raymond. 'He's just another kid at school, I’ve said that already.’

‘If you don’t tell me, I’m pulling the disco.’

‘Bulot!’ rattled Bernard.

‘But I’ve told you everything Monsieur,’ said Raymond. He was almost crying.

'Well tell me more. Tell me everything you know, however small the details. Think of it as a crime drama. Has he been wearing new clothes; does he have a new phone or computer? Has he been taking out girls to the cinema or for pizza?’

‘In Ventrèche?’ asked Raymond looking stunned. ‘Monsieur Mayor, have you been to Ventrèche recently?’

‘No,’ he said proudly.

‘The cinema closed down years ago,’ added Bernard.

‘Did it? Good. But that’s not important right now. Is there anything to suggest he's come into some money? This Macarthur fellow.’

‘Arthur you mean.’

‘Whoever!’

The Mayor was bright red now, and Miss Murs seriously feared she might lose her husband, and imagined people asking her that awkward question: ‘How long were you married before he passed away?’

'About six hours,' she would reply.

'Oh,' they would say. 'Really? How tragic.'

The Mayor continued. 'Is there anything to suggest he had come into some money?'

'Money?'

'Yes, money, Raymond. That stuff we will all go without including you if we don't find out why Le Glitch has mysteriously disappeared into thin air.'

Raymond shook his head. 'Monsieur Bulot,' he said. 'I honestly don't know anything.'

Jean Marc sat back on his seat and sluiced back another glass of wine in one. The days of being a tea drinker were well and truly over. 'Do you want my theory Raymond?'

'If you want.'

'Michel Arnold paid Kevin Macarthur, or whatever his name is, to change Le Glitch back to normal by some computer wizardry - How's that? Does that sound familiar?'

Raymond just laughed out loud.

'Funny eh?' yelled Jean Marc his eyes piercing into Raymond's large cranium.

'I'm sorry Monsieur Mayor,' said Raymond graciously. 'I'm not laughing at you, honest, it's just that there's no way on earth Kevin Arthur could have hacked into a satnav company. It's totally impossible in fact.'

'Why not,' Jean Marc demanded pouring another glass of wine.

'Because Kevin Arthur's a total idiot.'

'I thought you said he was a technical wizard,' Jean Marc said to Bernard.

'No I didn't,' Bernard retorted quickly. 'I said he was a technical wizard, or something.' He emphasised the word *something*. 'I remember it clearly.'

Jean Marc frowned. Bernard Clé, ever the pedant.

'Honestly Monsieur Mayor,' Raymond said calmly. 'Kevin Arthur couldn't tell a megabyte from a slice of pizza. He's as thick as a carpet. Anyone knows that. He only thinks he's clever because his dad was some computer genius. I mean *was*, now he's a total alcoholic.'

Jean Marc felt like a train had run through his head.

'I'm sorry, what did you say?' The Mayor's eyes were fixed firmly on the kid. Nobody else moved, all were mesmerised by the plot Raymond was weaving. Never in his whole life had so many people paid him such attention.

'His dad worked for a computer company,' the boy continued. 'I'm not sure which. Maybe it was Microsoft. Perhaps Apple. But it was years ago. In the 1990s or even 1980s. Now he's just a drunk.'

'Why didn't you say that before?' Jean Marc choked and nearly fell back off his chair and onto the limestone slabs of the village square.

'You didn't ask,' Raymond said coolly.

'You idiot Raymond.' It was Bernard this time. 'Why didn't you tell the Mayor that beforehand? What happens if we have to close the bar?'

Raymond scoffed. 'We managed quite well before,' he reminded his grandfather.

'Don't get shitty with me Raymond,' boomed Bernard. 'I may not be your father but I can clip you round the ear a few times.'

Jean Marc was smiling, that's more like it, he thought. A bit of discipline for once.

'If it fails, you'll have to go and live with your mum and dad again,' Bernard threatened.

'Right everyone.' Jean Marc stood up. 'The time for talking is over. We're off to storm Ventrèche; The Revolution has begun. And you're coming with us too Raymond. Tell us where this Monsieur Arthur lives. The fete is cancelled.'

Raymond broke into tears instantly.

'We're going nowhere!'

Now it was Miss Murs' turn to stand up. She was only five foot three, but she appeared to have grown a few inches in the last few seconds, and was now rising above the assembled crowd like an angel. 'It's my wedding day and it's Ray Gun's disco which he's done without fault for nearly ten years. We're going to eat up out Crêpes courtesy of Annette from Ventrèche. And then we will all dance and get very very drunk. We can deal with Ventrèche tomorrow.'

No!' Jean Marc boomed. 'Today!' But Francis immediately dragged him back down by his coattails.

'Jean Marc,' Francis ordered. 'As your best man, friend and deputy mayor, I order you to enjoy your wedding and get drunk with your friends and wife. We'll deal with Ventrèche in the morning. They are not going to go away, are they?'

After a couple of minutes of hard thought, he downed another glass of wine. 'Yes, you're right. I'm sorry Raymond,' he said to the crying boy. 'Spin those discs.'

Chapter 24 - The Hangover

The next morning Miss Murs and Jean Marc woke up hungover and married. 'Well that was a night to remember,' declared Miss Murs as she chased a packet of aspirin around the inside of the bedside table, still full of Jean Marc's model bicycles he made from steel wire over fifty-five years ago.

'I hardly remember any of it,' he confessed. 'Can't even remember coming to bed.'

'I noticed,' mumbled Miss Murs. 'Oh well, there's always tomorrow night.'

'What's that?'

'Oh nothing really, I was just thinking maybe we should wait in case Le Glitch was just a glitch and today it's back to normal. Save charging over to Ventrèche for no reason.'

Jean Marc was clutching his forehead and at the same time remembering doing the conga around the village square to the sound of Copacabana by Barry Manilow. A song he insisted Raymond play over and over again as he was convinced it would be the last time he would ever hear it when the demise of Le Glitch destroyed the village forever.

'No today is the day,' he pronounced firmly climbing out of bed and almost collapsing to the floor. 'God!' he complained. 'What was I drinking last night,' he said clutching his forehead again.

'About three bottles of Francis' 15% red Ventoux his friend brings over from Carpentras,' clarified Miss Murs.

'God, not that stuff again,' he choked, remembering his birthday. 'Feels like I've swallowed a hammer.'

'But I was thinking, what if this Colin Arthur fellow has nothing to do with it,' pleaded Miss Murs. 'And it's all been a big mistake. I mean we can't just go blundering in, we're not the police.'

'We're just paying him a visit that's all. Plus Miss Murs. Sorry Isabelle.' He had vowed to stop calling her Miss Murs. 'We have nothing to lose. Either we're right or we're wrong.'

'What happens if we are wrong?'

'Then we're wrong. Then we come back looking stupid as normal. I'm just a Mayor of a small-time village with nothing to lose. I heard that line in a Mel Gibson film. Or something like that anyway.'

Miss Murs had never heard of Mel Gibson. In her parents' house, it was the radio, cards or boring French literature like Balzac or Maupassant.'

'Plus Miss Murs, sorry Isabelle,' he corrected. 'There's nothing better to loosen a hangover than a good punch up. That's what Francis always used to say anyway after one of his monumental village benders.'

She nodded and remembered the shouting and insults and bawling in the square at dawn when she was growing up. Looking from her bedroom window and seeing dark shadows grappling with each other then falling over again, then getting up and fighting again. When she asked her father who they were he simply said, 'Italians. And Francis Conda. But he'll be dead soon.'

Miss Murs grinned to herself. Well Francis isn't dead. You're dead. So there!

'I think that's a great idea,' she hollered. 'Why not? Let's gather the troops and pitchforks.' At the age of fifty-two, the thought of intense violence suddenly seemed incredibly appealing.

'Great!' Jean Marc looked at his new wife in glowing adoration.

If he had known when he first saw Miss Murs emerging from her parents' house to collect the mail, aged five, that one day he would end up marrying her, he wouldn't have believed it. In fact he would have needed pinching with a pair of industrial jump leads they used down the mine when the machinery broke down.

'I'll go and wake up the Young Couple and they can drive us,' he said getting changed into his usual garb of espadrilles, cotton trousers and a white shirt.

'Why can't Madame Coquelicot drive us?'

'She always drives. Which is something we must sort out at some point. It's absurd that the only legal driver out of the six of us is Madame Coquelicot.'

This was true and another inescapable truth about the main players in this saga. Except for Madame Coquelicot, no one could drive. True Madame Coquelicot had never passed a driving test as such - the only requisite in her day was to drive in a straight line for a hundred metres without crashing into anything (which given her record, it was a surprise she passed). But she did and the fact remained that at ninety-two she was the only legal driver among the committee. Jean Marc had once been given the chance to learn by La Poste when it was motorising its fleet. But had refused on the grounds that the bicycle was man's greatest invention and therefore good enough for him (and La Poste). Francis had never had the need to drive, plus he was always drunk. Miss Murs had spent all her time looking after her parents. Albert had been refused on medical grounds, although, ironically, he was able to drive a tractor complete with razor sharp rotary mowing blades. Ethel had seen too many car accidents as a nurse. And Bernard Clé simply hadn't bothered.

This left the nimble and evergreen Madame Coquelicot to ferry in supplies from Ventrèche in a Suzuki Ignis her husband Cyrille used to drive. Which when fully laden with bread, potatoes, steak, flour, eggs, beer and wine scraped along the floor like a broken wheelbarrow.

'I agree, but I'm sure Magalie won't mind driving us today,' said Miss Murs. 'We don't want to bother the young couple again.'

'No, but we might need linguistic back up when we confront Colin Arthur. If his French is as crap as most expats living here, he'll probably still struggle to say Hello.'

Chapter 25 - Colin Arthur

Fifteen minutes later, Jean Marc Bulot, Isabelle Bulot, Albert Gramme, Francis Conda and the Young Couple were all outside Colin Arthur's house. A shabby whitewashed three-story townhouse in the centre of Ventrèche that from the front looked like the stodgy side of a vanilla slice. The moss-covered roof tiles and half collapsed chimney looked like they were about to crash into the house at any minute. In short, the house was a wreck and confirmed to the four Crêpians that Ventrèche was as derelict, diseased and as horrible as they had always thought.

'Hello,' finally came a muffled voice in English after a minute of Jean Marc incessantly ringing the bell.

'Monsieur Arthur,' thundered Jean Marc in true confrontational style. 'Open up!'

'Who are you?' came a terrified voice followed by a clinking of glass on glass behind the brown door.

'Don't worry Monsieur Arthur.' It was Miss Murs now, deciding a less aggressive tone might be needed. 'We're friends of Raymond Clé, your son Kevin goes to school with him. Could we have a few words?'

'What about?' came Colin Arthur. 'On a Sunday?'

'It's about Le Glitch,' said Miss Murs.

'The what?' came a puzzled voice.

'You know what we're talking about,' Jean Marc thundered again.

Miss Murs kicked her husband in the shin.

'What was that?' cried Colin Arthur. Obviously the man was a nervous wreck.

'Nothing, my husband's just stubbed his toe.' Then she turned to whisper loudly in her husband's ear. 'I thought we agreed on a conciliatory tone,' she hissed.

'Sorry,' Jean Marc whispered back. 'Something happens to me when I enter this village. It's like walking into hell - I start howling.'

'Pull yourself together Jean Marc,' she insisted.

'Monsieur Arthur,' he started again. 'We just want a few words on an inter-village matter.'

'What's that?'

'Cooperation between the villages of Gigot County to maximise economic growth on a micro level to create a macro interface to attract investment and diversity.'

'I think I got that pamphlet as well,' responded Colin Arthur laughing a bit. 'Gigot County Bulletin, wasn't it?'

'Err,' quivered Jean Marc feeling embarrassed. 'Not sure. But if you would only open the door, we might be able to speak a bit easier to each other. What do you say?'

Colin Arthur let out a large sigh from behind the door. Like the door of a fan oven being opened. 'What did you say it was about again. A glitch?'

From years of looking after her condescending and lying parents, Miss Murs was an expert in identifying when a person was telling the truth or not. So much of her life had been filled with deciphering her mother and father's lies that she was practically a master in covert espionage. When she heard Colin Arthur say the word 'glitch' the flatness in the 'i' sound plus no discernible rise in intonation towards the end of the word, indicated that unless he was a phenomenally good actor or indeed a master spy himself, he didn't have a clue what they were talking about.

She was about to convey her findings to her husband and argue it was a wasted trip and that they should leave immediately, when Colin Arthur opened the door.

Contrary to the impression she had built of him driving over, he was actually quite attractive. Yes, a bit dishevelled and scruffily dressed in a filthy roll top pullover and a pair of black jeans stained with something that made them appear shiny. And the smell from the house: canned sardines, old cake and alcohol, didn't lend to his appearance. But apart from that he was totally different to the geeky computer guy she'd imagined. In another world he might have been quite dashing.

Jean Marc didn't think so. 'Look Monsieur Arthur,' he blundered in. 'We're quite hungover, so we want to make this as painless as possible.'

Colin Arthur's eyes lit up at the word hangover. 'Please come in.'

'Thank you,' replied Jean Marc curtly. 'This is my wife Miss Murs.'

'Call me Isabelle,' she insisted quickly.

'The deputy Mayor of Crêpe, Francis Conda,' continued Jean Marc. 'Our groundsman Albert Gramme, and our lawyers from England.' He pointed to the Young Couple.

Miss Murs whispered defiantly to her husband. 'What on earth are you talking about? Lawyers?'

'It just came to me,' the Mayor whispered back as they tramped into his house. 'The illusion of power, I remember it from a film we watched recently.'

'I'm sorry, it's a bit of a mess,' apologised Colin Arthur once he had shown everyone to a seat in the dark lounge that smelt like a bar at closing time. 'If I'd known you were coming, I would have cleared up a bit.'

They looked around at an ocean of empty bottles littering the floor. Empty crisp packets and biscuit boxes populated the sofa and armchairs like rodents. Ready meal boxes, pizza trays and Chinese takeaway cartons were piled high in one corner like mini skyscrapers. A coffee table contained more glasses with dead moths and cigarette butts. The curtains were shut tight and the only table at the far end of the room had a giant white computer on it.

'It looks fine,' said Miss Murs diplomatically. 'I like the wallpaper.'

They all gazed at the red wallpaper with flecks of white paint like someone had flicked sour cream over it with a whisk. A gaudy reminder of some appalling 1970s decoration, which over forty years later no one had bothered to replace.

'Mmm,' said Colin Arthur as though he had never noticed it before. 'It came with the house.'

'Did the bottles?' jested Jean Marc.

'Some of them; some I've added,' Colin Arthur laughed, realising that despite the unannounced visit it might be nice to have some company for a change. 'So anyway, what can I do you for?'

'Do you for?' asked Jean Marc not understanding.

'It means how can I help you?' clarified the Young Man. 'It's a colloquial expression.'

'Oh.'

'We should be speaking French, shouldn't we?' apologised Colin Arthur. Then looked embarrassed. 'Been here fifteen years but still can't get the hang of it. French,' he added as though it was an extinct language.

'We can speak in English,' insisted Jean Marc. 'Albert and Francis speak a bit but not much.' He pointed to the two men on the opposite sofa. 'But they'll get the gist of it.'

'So why are you here?' asked Colin Arthur.

'What's going on between you and Michel Arnold?' said Jean Marc flatly.

'Michel Arnold?' Colin Arthur looked completely baffled. 'What that idiot mayor?

'Yes, that idiot Mayor.'

'Why do you think I've got anything to do with him?' Colin Arthur carried on. 'I can't stand the man prancing around in his cowboy shirts. Thinks he's God's answer to woman, but you should see the state of his wife, looks like he married one of his horses.'

Jean Marc was about to wrap one of his empty whisky bottles round his head but Miss Murs grabbed his arm.

'So you've never talked to Michel Arnold?' said Miss Murs quickly pulling her husband back.

'Well yeah of course I've talked to him,' responded Colin Arthur. 'I sometimes work for him.'

'Ah-ha,' cried Jean Marc. 'I thought so.'

'Arnold came to see me about three weeks ago,' said Colin Arthur pouring neat whiskey into a highball. 'There was a problem with the internet in the Town Hall. Maybe he called it a glitch, I'm not sure. Said it would take years for the prefecture in Gigot to get round to fixing it so he came to me. Said he would pay me two hundred Euros for the trouble, cash. Drink anyone?'

Francis came to attention immediately even though he hadn't understood a word. 'Oui!' he frothed.

'Help yourself, sorry I should have offered,' Colin Arthur said in flawless French. Clearly when it came to the rudiments of ordering and serving alcohol, he was fluent. 'Anyone else?'

'I think we're alright,' quacked Jean Marc, who had gone extremely pale and looked like he'd been sucked into space by Colin Arthur's news. 'On the other hand, yes I'll have one.'

'Whisky?'

Jean Marc nodded. 'Let's get this straight. You don't work for him in any other capacity?'

'Nah I hate the bastard. But if he asks me to repair the computer system and he's paying cash, I'm in. I've done it a few times for him over the years.'

'But how do you converse with him?' demanded Jean Marc sensing a hole in Colin Arthur's story. 'I know for a fact he doesn't speak English.'

'I know enough French,' countered Colin Arthur. 'Moreover, computer speak is pretty much the same in any language.'

'I owe you an apology then, Monsieur Arthur,' confessed Jean Marc. 'I'm sorry.'

Colin Arthur shrugged in true British fashion that spelt I couldn't really give a fuck, as long as I've a drink in my hand. 'We all make mistakes mate,' he said giving the Mayor his whisky.

Everybody had a long slug of their drinks and then Jean Marc explained the story of Le Glitch so far. Without missing out of course, not that it was relevant to the tale, that Michel Arnold's horse of a wife was in fact Jean Marc's ex-wife.

'Oh,' groaned Colin Arthur looking into his drink. 'Well I owe you an apology as well, I didn't know she was your wife.'

'Ex-wife,' chipped in Miss Murs. 'I think she looked better when she was younger.'

'I'm sure she did,' agreed Colin Arthur.

'We better be going then,' stammered Jean Marc standing up.

'But wait,' said Colin Arthur, a glint in his alcohol ravaged eye. 'This Glitch you talk about.' He said it in an Arthurian legend tone. 'I might be able to help.'

Chapter 26 - Twelve bottles of whisky

An hour later they were still at Colin Arthur's house listening to him and Francis discuss the vast range of whiskies available in France these days. Some inbuilt telepathic bond alcoholics possess where the ability to speak each other's language when discussing ways to obliterate oneself simply wasn't necessary.

Jean Marc had heard a lot of accents over the summer - Geordie, Scouse, Cockney, Cider Country, Yorkshire - and had gotten quite good at deciphering them and placing their locations. But he couldn't place Colin Arthur's and it took him a few more whiskies to realise Colin Arthur was not English at all. But Scottish.

'Born and bred in Perthshire,' he said with pride waving the bottle of Teachers around like a sabre. Before going on to recite his life story.

At school he had been a maths prodigy and got a scholarship to study computer science at Edinburgh University. A highly specialised subject at the time studied by men who lived off Weetabix and wore thick black canvas jackets even in the middle of summer.

But after a term Colin Arthur was bored with university life, and on an impulse fled to San Francisco and got a job for a small computer software company. Word got around that this Scottish guy was good and soon Colin Arthur was headhunted by Apple Corp to work for them as a programmer. After ten years he set up his own software business in London, writing stock ordering programs for supermarkets, and made a fortune.

'Retail computing was where the real money was at in the early nineties,' Colin Arthur said. 'Huge supermarket expansion in the UK meant efficient ordering software was absolutely vital and they would pay big money to developers to get the best system to give them an edge over their rivals. Programmes that could crunch numbers to see who bought what, where and when. That's why we all carry those stupid loyalty cards that pretend to save us money when really it's just a copy of our shopping list on their files.

'Have you ever been to your local supermarket and been slightly amazed that more or less what you want is always there? Sometimes right in front of you when you walk into the store. To the point where it's not you who decides what you want for dinner, but the supermarket.'

'I can't believe that!' cried the girl. 'That's just cynical.'

'Cynical but true my dear. Check it out next time you go to your local store. I bet you that you walk home not with the bag of sausages you came for, but with a bag of sausages the supermarket thinks you might like. And guess what? They were probably on offer too! Trust me, I know how it works, I practically wrote the manual.'

'I'll mention your ideas to Ethel Budd,' laughed Jean Marc.

'Who's Ethel Budd?' asked Colin Arthur.

'She runs the village shop,' replied Miss Murs.

'There are no offers there I can tell you that,' barked the Mayor. 'Even the out of date stuff is full price. Not that she has much. Ten things at the last count. Beer, Beans, Pasta, Rice, Potatoes, Cornflakes, Milk, Brown Sauce, Marmalade and Fray Bentos pies. Everything at airport prices and yet everyone buys them, she must be a millionaire by now.'

'The old campsite shop dilemma,' mused Colin Arthur.

'What's that?' asked The Young Man, who was scribbling away.

'Well, you can either buy your milk there at inflated prices, or travel ten miles down the road to buy it. By which time your tea is cold. What do you do? I'll tell you what you do. You buy the milk for a pound a pint because you're too hungover to drive into town.

'And the great thing about these kinds of shops are, the owners don't need to do much to attract business because it's already there. In the retail business it's called leeching. Wait until some other schmuck puts in all the hard work advertising, promo work, getting the people in, then rock up and reap the rewards. Looks like this Ethel Budd is a real smart dude.'

Jean Marc was grinding his teeth. He hated to admit it, but he was right. 'So anyway, Monsieur Arthur, this is all very interesting,' he scoffed. 'But what we want to know is, what happened to you? In other words, how come you ended up in Ventrèche?'

'Ah well. I broke,' Colin Arthur started swirling the amber liquid in the glass. 'Not a break down in the traditional sense. It didn't feel mental, more physical. I just broke. Like a needle on a record player snapping. I hadn't stopped for twenty years and one day in the office I collapsed and couldn't move. I felt electrocuted like someone had whipped me with a cattle prod or a Taser gun. I managed to shout for help and spent the next few days in hospital. I was soon released and given the all clear. Exhaustion they said. But when I got back to work, I had no fight left in me, the spark had gone and all I wanted to do was drift from one bar to the next until I phoned a taxi to take me home. This continued for years and I lost my wife, my house, my business and yet I couldn't give a shit. My mind was uncoiling and all the crap I had ever learnt was spewing out of the top like a Roman Candle, you remember those?'

The young couple nodded.

'The thing is I didn't want the uncoiling to stop. It was great. I felt like something was happening in my head. I didn't give a shit so I just drank. Drinking all day and hooking up with girls. Having a ball. To hell with being a computer geek, I thought. Now I was a character in all the books I used to read. Bukowski, Kerouac, Burroughs, you know them?'

The Young Man was nodding.

'Sitting in bars watching the world gently go to shit and doing nothing about it because I was so drunk. What's that Pink Floyd song? Comfortably Numb. Yeh, that's what I was, comfortably numb, and it only stopped when I bought four cracked ribs, a dislocated shoulder, a fractured pelvis, two broken arms and a smashed-up face after an appointment with a couple of thugs in some bar.'

'I know it sounds like it's straight out of a film, but it's true. But when I got out of the hospital, again, I decided my time of being a Bo-Ho drunk was over when a friend recommended a rehab clinic in Glasgow, of all places. "They have great facilities there for that kind of thing," I remember him telling me.'

'I went there and after four months I came here to Ventrèche.' The assembled crowd looked at him like he was absolutely nuts. 'You came to Ventrèche?' said the Young Man.

'It was a strange choice I admit but I just needed some peace and quiet and countryside. And as it happened the same friend who recommended the rehab clinic had moved to Gigot with his family after spending four years in prison for tax fraud, he was a lawyer.'

'He put me up for a few weeks until I got a flat and I started working online doing consultancy work for startup tech companies. Easy money and soon I had enough money for a house here in Ventrèche.'

His eyes rolled around his sockets showing us the room. 'Life was good, I met Caroline at a science fair in Lyon - she was a teacher - we had Kevin and all was good. Then a few years ago she left me for a restaurant owner in Gigot, taking my boy with her. After sixteen years sober, I hit the booze again. Big time.' He said big time like it was a hamburger. 'And here I am. A mess.'

'God,' sighed Jean Marc. 'What horrible luck. Losing your wife to a restaurant owner in Gigot.'

Miss Murs squeezed his hand tightly. 'What he means is, what a terrible thing.'

But Colin Arthur smiled. Despite the Mayor's impatience, he liked him. He liked his abruptness. 'An Italian as well,' Colin Arthur laughed sloshing more whisky into his glass like he was watering a plant.

Jean Marc screwed up his face. 'Terrible,' he announced. 'Probably one of the miners.'

'Miners?'

'Don't you know about the mine? We had miners from the Abruzzi.'

Colin Arthur shook his head. 'I never knew.'

'Never heard of the famous story of Paulo?'

Colin Arthur looked blank.

Jean Marc's face lit up. He hadn't told this story for years. Ever since a German family arrived in the dead of winter so lost, they weren't even sure if they were still in France. Luckily Miss Murs calmed them down with strong mulled wine before they drove off to Ventrèche half drunk after passing up on Jean Marc's suggestion of sleeping in the Town Hall on camp beds.

'It was the last recorded crime in Crêpe over thirty years ago,' Jean Marc started the story. 'One of the last Italian miners, Paulo, stole the previous Mayor's wife's handbag and tried to bolt it back to The Abruzzi. Only he got snagged by the Gendarmes at Gigot train station after a twenty-kilometre tramp across the muddy fields in freezing rain just as he was about to board a train for Milan. They let him off in the end as long he signed a document promising he would never return to the region again. The Italian couldn't believe his luck. So he signed with a large 'X' and left as quickly as possible. They even gave him a couple of sandwiches and a bottle of beer for the journey.'

'I wonder if he ever made it back home?' asked Colin Arthur curiously.

'He did,' confirmed the Mayor. 'The previous Mayor before me, Maurice Lafarge, received a letter from his mother apologising for her son's disgraceful behaviour and promising that it would never happen again now he was back in the beautiful rolling hills of The Abruzzi. She finished off by saying that he was much happier now and that living in Crêpe all those years had nearly killed him.'

'What rubbish,' offered Colin Arthur. 'Crepe is a lovely village and I love your terracotta pots on the limestone slabs. Very stylish. Very Italian in fact.'

'You've been?' asked a surprised Mayor.

'Oh yeah, a few times, over the summer, Le Restaurant anyway. Cheap wine I was told. Lovely steaks as well. Very meaty.'

'Really?' said Miss Murs. 'Why didn't you say anything?'

Arthur shrugged.

'Oh well, I'm glad you enjoyed it,' she said.

‘Which,’ grandstanded the Mayor, ‘is why we’re so keen to get this Glitch back. Which now we've covered your life story, it's where you come in.'

‘Ah yes.’ Colin Arthur let a few drops of whisky drip on his filthy floor and looked very thoughtful. Then he paced the room for a few minutes. ‘It's most likely a Random ReDirectional Rerouting - RaRR for short.’

‘A what?' creaked Jean Marc.

'Occasionally the atomic clocks onboard the Global Positioning Satellites miss a beat causing the timing of the whole network to be fractionally altered. I mean I’m talking absolute nanoseconds here. Almost nothing. But on the ground, this adds up to perhaps a few metres. Sometimes more. On occasions this sends the motorist off on an alternative route. In this case, instead of sending motorists along the bypass to Ventrèche, it nudges them left a bit and puts them on the old road which goes through Crêpe. And from what you've told me, because there's no road sign in Crêpe, when they arrive in Crêpe, they think they’ve arrived in Ventrèche.'

'Yes,' creaked the Mayor looking at Albert, who was asleep.

‘How do we get it back?’ pleaded Miss Murs.

Colin Arthur paused. A long lengthy pause filling the room with stifling tension. ‘You can’t,’ he finally admitted. ‘I’m sorry. The atomic clocks must have been recalibrated by the satellite company. It's impossible to undo them.'

'Can’t they be undone at all?’ asked the Young Man busy taking notes.

‘Impossible,’ Colin Arthur declared. 'You could move the entire village a few kilometres towards the bypass, that might work.' It was meant as a joke, but the Mayor wasn't in the mood.

‘I'm sorry,' declared Colin Arthur. 'But look, I'll try.’

'You just said it was impossible,' snapped Jean Marc.

'They said the four-minute mile was impossible. But it was done.'

'Can it be done?' Jean Marc pressed.

'I mean technically, yes,' stated Colin Arthur. 'But you would have to be a genius to get through all the firewalls and security traps.'

'I thought you were a genius,' the Mayor reminded him.

Colin Arthur shrugged weakly. 'Well, maybe, but even if I managed it, it wouldn't take long for the various national security agencies to be alerted that someone was fiddling with their satellites and before we know it there's a missile through our window.' Colin Arthur made the sound effect of an explosion like a seven-year-old boy playing with a plastic spaceship.

'Bit far fetched, isn't it?' the Young Man guffawed.

'So you can at least try then?' hurried the Mayor of Crêpe now tiring of this drunkard Scot whose theories on *Le Glitch* were now veering into the realms of fantasy. Jean Marc wanted facts not half-baked sci-fi thought up by writers who were all as whacked out as Colin Arthur was.

'Maybe when I was younger,' he reminisced, 'but not now.' He took another glug. 'I'm not much use for anything these days.'

'How much?' Jean Marc asked flatly.

'How much what?' replied Colin Arthur, frowning heavily

'How much do you want?'

Miss Murs shifted uneasily in her chair.

'For what?'

'For correcting *Le Glitch*. Come on, we've all got a price. What's yours?' Jean Marc demanded.

Colin Arthur looked genuinely baffled. 'I'm sorry Jean Marc, I'm not with you.'

'I'll give you 5000 Euros to fix *Le Glitch*, it's all I've got.'

'Just a minute,' cut in Miss Murs seeing those Hawaiian sandy beaches disappear up in smoke. 'Shouldn't we talk about it first.'

'There's nothing to talk about,' boomed Jean Marc. 'I'll sacrifice my holiday for the sake of my village.'

'How about my holiday,' complained Miss Murs. 'I've never been on holiday.'

The Young Couple were nearly weeping. Never in their lives had they witnessed such real-life drama, such sacrifice.

'I'm prepared to pay whatever the rate is to save our village - so name it!'

Even Colin Arthur looked close to tears. He too thought this kind of honour, where someone would sacrifice a dream holiday for the sake of a dusty village, was a thing of the past.

'Monsieur Mayor,' announced Colin Arthur. 'I don't want your money, take your wife on holiday for God's sake.'

'Thank you,' said Miss Murs, glaring at Jean Marc.

'Look, I'll tell you what,' he continued. 'I'll have a look at the Glitch, see what I can do, but I must warn you I can't guarantee anything. It might be too tricky, but I'll have a go.'

'Fair do's,' said Jean Marc remembering the expression Ethel Budd used all the time. 'But if you need anything, just ask.'

'Crate of Teachers might come in handy,' Colin Arthur stated.

'Done!' bellowed Jean Marc, realising twelve bottles of whisky was considerably less than five grand. 'When can you start?'

'Now.' He jumped up and fell over like a child tripping over a toy tractor.

'Maybe wait until tomorrow,' suggested Miss Murs kindly.

‘I think you’re right,’ accepted Colin Arthur still lying on the floor. And with that they left and let Colin Arthur do battle with his demons and Crêpe's much-needed Glitch.

Chapter 27 - Microwave Meals

Jean Marc rolled over in his bed and dreaded the day. It was now the third week of September and there was still no news from Colin Arthur who they presumed dead.

They had phoned him every other day but had received a garbled answer machine message telling the caller that: 'Life is meaningless, but if you want to leave a message, do so after the annoying beep and I might get back to you if I can be bothered.'

'We are never going to get to Hawaii, are we?' moaned the Mayor to Miss Murs.

'I could sell my house,' said Miss Murs.

The Mayor looked at his wife. She looked pale. The result of the ready meals they'd become addicted to ever since seeing them littered around Colin Arthur's pigsty of a house. An orgy of reheated tartiflette, TV game shows and badly dubbed American police shows had made the past few weeks speed by. Their meals heated up in the old microwave the Town Hall had bought in the mid-nineties and that had somehow found its way into Jean Marc's flat. The ancient Panasonic radiating their kidneys to medium-rare as it whirred round another supermarket Coq-Au-Vin.

'But who would buy it, Isabelle? It's worthless. Brits won't touch a thing any more with all this Brexit nonsense going on. And French people want nothing to do with the countryside any more. May as well airbrush it from existence. And anyway, as we've discussed, money isn't the actual problem Isabelle, is it?'

'What is it then?' she asked looking like a person who really needed a holiday.

'We've been through this before. We can probably get the money together. I have some savings and I could borrow some from Francis - he's got stacks from God knows where. Bernard might even throw us a few coins if we need it.'

'But why can't we just go for God's sake? We could simply go and come back like everyone else does when they go on holiday.'

'Because we couldn't. I can't go knowing we are coming back to this. Go away on the holiday of our lives with everything falling around us. The village, Francis, Bernard, Ethel Budd. It wouldn't be right Isabelle. Even now the thought of a Pina Colada turns my stomach.'

'They probably do other drinks,' suggested Miss Murs attempting to lighten the mood.

'You don't understand Isabelle.' He had now got used to calling her Isabelle. 'All my life I've been indifferent to civic life, doing things for the greater good, for the sake of the community. I'm a postman Isabelle. We are all the same. Self-centred, self-righteous and highly unambitious. All postmen know that. It's why they stay in the job for forty years posting love letters and postcards and bills and demands. Doing the same stupid rounds in the same village where they were born and where they will die. They are a bunch of morons.

'And yet now, I see the good in everything and everyone. Even in that ratface Michel Arnold. Even Francis,' he added half smirking. 'We are all working together for the greater good. Before, I saw Albert and Francis and Madame Coquelicot as useless ornaments in a junk shop waiting to be thrown away. Dusty bric-a-brac no one cared about. Now I see them as the vital cogs in an incredible social machine. The machine being The Crêpe Catering Committee.

‘Remember when you were a child, building sandcastles by the sea, Isabelle.’

Miss Murs had never been to the sea but she imagined what it might be like. Then remembered neither had Jean Marc, he must be daydreaming, so she said ‘Yes.'

‘You prepare the groundwork, bulldoze the sand up with your hands and then create the castle with your fingers and discarded lollipop sticks. Then you stand back and admire your masterpiece, only to be called for lunch by your parents. You cry and fret as you watch the tide come in and you want to build barriers to protect your creation. But your parents get mad and insist you come for lunch beyond the dunes. When you return half an hour later, your castle is destroyed and you sink down to your knees in despair. That's how I feel.'

'But you've never been to the sea.'

'I don't need to. I know what despair feels like.'

Miss Murs rolled her eyes at her husband’s propensity for excessive melodrama.

Jean Marc was rubbing his kidneys and was about to say something but Miss Murs cut in.

‘Let’s go and see Monsieur Arthur right now,' she declared.

'What, now?' Jean Marc said gazing around the sitting room. When he had asked Miss Murs to marry him, he had no idea she was so messy. It was like living with a teenager. Before it had always been clean and tidy. Now, a month into married life it resembled a hovel, with crisp packets, empty chicken cartons, and wine bottles littering the room. It was actually starting to look like Colin Arthur's.

Chapter 28 - Colin Arthur Revisited

'Arthur, you drunk!' bellowed Jean Marc outside the Scotsman's door twenty minutes later. 'When are you going to fix this Glitch?

'Just a minute,' came a voice and the familiar clink of bottles being cleared. Jean Marc and Miss Murs looked at each other conjuring up their own vision of what the place looked like.

'Hi,' said Colin Arthur opening the door a few minutes later trying to look like he'd been at his desk since seven o'clock in the morning. 'Glad you came round. Come in.' He ushered Jean Marc and Miss Murs into the dark lounge.

On the floor were discarded plates of half eaten ready meals left to rot. More bottles lying on their side and dirty highball glasses containing dried whisky. It made their place looked pristine.

'It's a bit of a mess,' he admitted after fixing himself and his guests a coffee. A pathetic token gesture to try and persuade them he had not been drinking solidly for a week but had in fact been working.

'So, how are we getting on?' Jean Marc asked tentatively.

'Good,' he said, drinking his coffee rather too quickly which Jean Marc bet was half full of whisky.

'Well, we're not,' the Mayor declared flatly. 'The village is still as dead as a cemetery at night and my residents are getting twitchy. Business is bad, Monsieur Arthur. Have you cracked it yet?'

'Err, not quite.'

'Which means you haven't started by the state of the place.'

'I'm undertaking preliminary research. It's not as simple as switching on a microwave you know,' stated Colin Arthur.

'Well you've been having plenty of practice at that,' Jean Marc remarked painfully, looking at the plates.

'Do you have any idea Monsieur Mayor what hacking into a multinational computer system entails, mmm?'

Jean Marc Bulot normally had an answer for most scenarios, but not this one. 'I have to say Monsieur Arthur, I wouldn't know where to start.'

'Good. Let me tell you. First you have to write new software to bypass the company's security system. This takes ages. Meanwhile on the other side of the fence, in other words in the offices of the company you are trying to hack into, there is a bank of highly intelligent hackers writing software to counter the software I've just written. And on it goes until I give up, drink myself to death, shoot myself, or am cleverer enough to outwit them.'

'Oh.' Was all the Mayor could manage.

'It's a game of chess. Or if you want it in layman's terms, a penalty shootout. Only in this penalty shootout the goal is shrunk to the size of a pinhead while moving around very quickly indeed. Or like one of those fairground shooting galleries where the sights are bent on purpose to stop you hitting the bull's-eye. The chances of winning are virtually zero. Does that make sense to you Monsieur Mayor?'

Jean Marc looked at the floor as he always did when he was defeated. 'Why are you bothering then?' the Mayor asked rather forlornly.

'Because there's a chance. Same as why people mindlessly do lotteries in the faintest of faintest hope, they might win a tenner. A reason to live if you like. It's either that or watch TV. Or get pissed.' He looked at his glass.

'And if you're thinking about why the place is such an utter mess, it's because I've been working twenty-two hours a day trying to crack your bloody Glitch. And yes, before you ask, I'm pissed. Why? I don't know. I work better that way. Would the Rolling Stones have made Exile on Main Street sober? I doubt it.' Jean Marc and Miss Murs had no idea what he was talking about. Exile on Main Street? Was he talking about Crêpe?

'Well, it's a good job we didn't bring you twelve bottles of Perrier then instead of whisky,' the Mayor joked.

Colin Arthur jumped out of his chair. 'You brought more whisky!'

'Of course,' exclaimed Miss Murs. 'The Mayor was against it, but I thought you might want a top up.'

'Thank you very much Isabelle,' said Colin Arthur. 'And please, call me Colin.'

Jean Marc frowned. It was Madame Bulot to him, not Isabelle.

'OK, Arthur,' he said, preferring to stick with the name he knew. 'I'm sure you're doing your best and I don't care if you drink yourself to death, it's not my concern, maybe your son's.' He paused. 'But that's not my business either. What is my business is my village, so if you could try, I would be most grateful. And yes, there's another twelve bottles in my boot - we'll bring them in. Unless you want to switch to Perrier?'

Colin Arthur seemed to think about it for a split second before replying: 'I think I'll stick to the Scotch if you don't mind.'

Chapter 29 - Crêpes this way!

When they got back to Crêpe later that afternoon something dawned on Miss Murs of great importance. It had in fact been there all summer, buzzing like a malicious insect at the back of her head. The key to Crêpe's success, wasn't the Glitch, but something stronger. Something more tangible than a computer program or satellites lost in space.

Despite Miss Murs' humble and limited life in Crêpe, she had always tried to think sideways rather than in a straight line, if only to divert herself from the maddening mundanity of her own life. All along they had been trying to solve the problem by hitting it with a digital hammer way up in space. What they needed was a real hammer, some nails and some paint.

'We don't need Le Glitch,' Miss Murs yelled out to the Young Girl who was carrying a stack of beer boxes from Bar La Boucle. In the preceding weeks the Young Couple, Francis, Bernard and Ethel Budd had drunk Bar La Boucle dry. As a result, the previously young looking couple had become the Middle Aged Couple.

'It's funny, because I was thinking the same thing the other day,' agreed the Young Girl. 'You've got a really good village here.'

'Yes yes yes,' Miss Murs screamed, 'That's what I've been saying. A simple sign on the bypass might do the trick.'

'Oh yes. The old-fashioned way. Bugger all this social media, review site lark. Back to the real world.'

'Exactly,' said Miss Murs. 'And also, we just need to stop worrying about getting one over on Ventrèche.'

'What is it with him and Ventrèche anyway?' asked the Young Girl.

'Jean Marc has got it into his head that the demise of Crêpe is Ventrèche's fault. Ever since that stupid football match and then the closure of the post office. He was a postman, you know.'

'Ah,' said the Young Man, who had sauntered up, pint in hand, wondering what all the oohing-and-ahhing was about. 'Well that explains everything. My father was one as well and he hated change. Scared of even the slightest variation in delivery routes or workloads. Had them up in arms. Strikes and walkouts. Terribly lazy man he was.'

'There you go,' said Miss Murs. 'Then you know what we are up against.'

'They're hard nuts to crack, postmen.'

'Tell me about it,' sighed Miss Murs as she watched her husband walk towards them carrying a box of bottles. 'Jean Marc,' she said when he was in earshot. 'Where can we get some paints and brushes from?'

'Brushes?' he said. 'Paints? Miss Murs, what on earth for? It's not the time to take up painting. We've got a war to win.'

Miss Murs turned to the Young Couple/Middle Aged couple. 'See!' Then turned back to her husband. 'We've decided to go it alone. We don't need the Glitch and we certainly don't need Ventrèche, Michel Arnold or Colin Arthur. And don't call me Miss Murs, I'm not your secretary any more, I'm your wife.'

'Sorry Isabelle. But what are you talking about? I've just bought another twelve more bottles of Teachers for that drunk Arthur from Ethel Budd's ridiculously expensive shop.'

'I thought you just gave him twelve.'

'This is twelve more to keep him going. Like a carrot. I'm putting everything into getting this Glitch back Miss Murs, so don't tell me we don't need it. Tell Ethel Budd that. She's as terrified as me that the end of the Glitch might destroy her business too - and I don't blame her given how much she charges. She could probably be banged up for extortion.'

'But don't you see Jean Marc.' It was the Young Girl who had become as maddened as Miss Murs with this inane and pointless battle with Ventrèche. 'We don't need the Glitch. We just need ourselves. Crêpe.'

'But Crêpe's just a tiny village in the middle of nowhere. Le Glitch was our saviour from God.'

'Don't be absurd, Jean Marc,' cried his wife. 'You're not religious.'

'We all turn religious in times of need Miss Murs. It's a well-known psychological fact.'

'Rome wasn't built in a day,' pleaded the Young Man. 'Once it was simply a tinpot village like this. Everything has to start from somewhere. You have to give it time to blossom.' He was speaking in clichés, but he knew Jean Marc loved clichés.

'Now we've planted the seed we can let it grow. Just imagine one day Jean Marc you might be Caesar.'

'Now you put it like that,' said Jean Marc puffing his chest out. There was nothing like being compared to a Roman Emperor to inflate a man's ego.

'Let's do a two-pronged attack then, like a pincer movement,' suggested the Young Man. 'We'll do the signs and some advertising and you take care of Colin Arthur. If it all fails it's only cost you twelve bottles of Teachers.'

‘Thirty-six actually,’ confirmed the Mayor. ‘I’ve already bought him twenty-four. Which at Ethel Budd’s shop amounts to almost a million euros. In old Francs at least.’

‘Still,’ smiled the Young Man. ‘It’s worth it. What do you say?’

Jean Marc liked the Young Man. He had some class and style and the Mayor had a vision of them settling here, maybe one day he could be Mayor and his children after that.

‘OK,’ proclaimed the Mayor. ‘Ask Albert for some painting equipment. But I’m still not letting go of the Glitch. I don’t know why, but for some reason it feels like I created it, I feel close to it. That morning in April looking out of the window, feeling like there was nothing to live for and then that car. That navy-blue Ford Galaxy appearing out of the mirage. Then the man, Cassidy was his name, and his wife telling me I should renovate the guesthouse. Then that kid, the one with the phone telling me there was nothing here in Crêpe. And then all of this happened.’ He stopped and looked at Miss Murs or rather Mrs Bulot, his wife, and he had a tear in his eye.

‘I feel like this happened for a reason and I don’t want to lose it. Call me old and sentimental but Le Glitch feels like the son I never see any more. I lost Jacques, but I don’t want to lose this one.

'God!' Miss Murs secretly cursed into her hanky. 'What a bloody drama queen.'

Chapter 30 - No Man's Land

The road signs were a total failure. Within days they had blown down. When the village replaced them, they were stolen, probably by Michel Arnold and his Gendarmes. After the fourth batch, they gave up and got drunk.

Then they got a phone call.

‘Could you come over?’

Without even listening to what Colin Arthur had to say, Jean Marc and Miss Murs were knocking on his door in Ventrèche. They were of course expecting to go through the same routine of waiting while he cleared a path to the door through a million clinking bottles.

Instead Colin Arthur answered the door clean shaven, wearing fresh clothes and a healthy-looking smile. Jean Marc and Miss Murs were so shocked they thought they’d gone to the wrong house.

'Greetings,' Colin Arthur said in his Scottish twang, which seemed to be less pronounced than normal.

‘*Bonjour*,' said the Mayor showing himself into the front room.

‘Come in,’ said Colin Arthur sarcastically. 'Be my guest.'

‘Thank you,’ replied Jean Marc nervously, 'wouldn't mind one of those whiskeys of yours.'

'Ah, can't help you there I'm afraid,' he replied sheepishly as though he had done something wrong. 'I decided to clean up my act a bit. Had a good look in the mirror and didn't like what I saw. So I knocked the booze on the head.'

'Well you look better,' smiled Miss Murs.

'I thought you said you worked better drunk,' commented the Mayor.

'Nah,' scoffed Colin Arthur. 'That's just a drunk's story. Denial. Once I stopped drinking and got to work on this Glitch of yours, I felt seriously better. And I needed to as well. In the old days any idiot with a ZX Spectrum and half a brain could hack into a mainframe. I mean, I did and I wasn't even that good, not compared to some guys I knew. Some of them could reprogramme the whole of the NASA space programme using a calculator. Geniuses they were. Nowadays you need to be Mossad trained to hack into something as simple as email. The security is immense.'

Miss Murs and Jean Marc eyeballed each other. Both thinking they might actually have preferred the old Colin Arthur: that drunken wreck of a man sloshing whisky and falling over the place. Now he had turned into some boring happy-clappy geek who drank barley tea and ate nuts for breakfast.

'Well anyway Colin,' cut in Jean Marc before he bored them all to death with memories of all-night coding sessions in San Francisco. 'I don't mean to be rude, but have you fixed this glitch or not?'

'I'm coming to that. But first, do you remember the story you told me about the young couple's map? And then the boy, the Cassidy boy? Both times Crêpe wasn't on the map they said.'

'Both idiots as well. Neither could read maps. In my day we were taught to navigate across streams and rivers and mountains using the Sun and a piece of string.'

Miss Murs looked at her husband trying to remember when this survival course happened and who took it. Certainly not Madame Coquelicot. She came to the conclusion that her husband was at times an inveterate liar.

'These days,' he continued, 'the youth of today wouldn't know a compass from a frying pan.'

'I agree Monsieur Mayor,' Colin Arthur said politely. 'However, on this occasion, they both appear to be right.'

'A snot-faced kid and a F. Scott Fitzgerald look-alike?'

'I find it hard to believe as well,' jested Colin Arthur. 'But they're right. I've checked many times and you don't appear to be on any map.'

'We're on the Gigot County Bulletin's map,' Miss Murs reminded him blithely.

He wasn't sure if it was an attempt at a joke or she was simply stating a mere fact. 'That's true,' Colin Arthur admitted cordially. 'But the fact is, except for that one, Crêpe, for reasons I can't explain, is not on any other known map in existence.'

'Are you sure, Arthur?'

'Yep,' he said sympathetically.

Jean Marc shrugged. 'So what? I bet there are Andean outposts that aren't on the map either. It's not the end of the world.'

'But it is.' Colin Arthur took his glasses off. A sure sign things were about to get serious. 'I'm not sure you're understanding me Monsieur. With all due respect to both of you. What I mean is, you're not on The Map.'

'What map?' Jean Marc was getting impatient as he always did around this ratty house in Ventrèche. 'The Magna Carta?'

'Close,' Colin Arthur admitted. 'What I mean is, you're not on Google.' He let the word Google resonate around the house as though it had spiritual meaning. 'Which for all intent and purpose for the majority of people on Planet Earth, bar the odd nutcase still roaming around with maps made by Charlemagne trying to find hidden treasure, is the modern day Magna Carta.'

'How about MapsMe, or OpenStreet or ViaMichelin?' suggested Miss Super Practical as normal. 'Are we on them?'

Colin Arthur was shaking his head. 'I checked all of them, Miss Murs. Look.' He flicked on his computer and the familiar triangle of nothing came up on the digital display in between Gigot, Ventrèche and Plante.

'Bloody hell,' screamed the Mayor like he was looking at a ghost. 'It's horrible.' And averted his eyes. 'That blankness.'

'And just to prove a point.' The computer boffin typed something. 'Here is *El Refugio de Puta Madre* - a remote mountain outpost on the Bolivian/Peruvian border.'

They looked at a red flashing dot with a few photos some intrepid explorer had added. 'And as you can see, there's life.' He tapped the screen gently.

'Albert was right,' Jean Marc muttered, remembering Crêpe's Tourist Trader listing.

'This is the Global Positioning Satellite Network Map from which all other maps are taken, more or less. I've set this to the highest scale meaning if you're not on here, you're not anyway. Trust me, I've checked every possible online and paper map and you're simply not on it.'

Jean Marc lowered his eyes; he could no longer look. All these years, he had tried, or half tried at least, when all this time *El Refugio de Puta Madre* - a sonofabitch icy hellhole stuck in the middle of nowhere - was more visible to the world than Crêpe. No wonder no one had ever visited.

'But how did this happen?' groaned Jean Marc. 'I mean this is a fucking joke, isn't it?'

'Yes,' agreed Colin Arthur. 'It is a fucking joke and I could speculate on why, but it would lead us into the realms of science-fiction.'

'Don't bother,' said the Mayor. 'I hate science fiction. Plus I'm not in the mood. But in short Arthur, you haven't fixed the Glitch at all.'

'No, I was going to tell you over the phone, but you hung up. I'm sorry.'

'It's not your fault,' the Mayor moaned. 'I jump to conclusions all the time. I've always been like that. Once as a postman I assumed old Jacques Boise had died because he hadn't answered his door for three days in a row, so I simply didn't bother to deliver his mail. When my boss summoned me to explain why the old man hadn't received any mail for months, it turned out he had simply been on holiday. I mean it's the most obvious thing in the world, but for some reason I jumped to the stupid conclusion he was dead. Maybe because he was old. Maybe because I'd never been on holiday. And now probably never will.'

Miss Murs bit her lip.

'And are you sure you've got nothing to drink? Petrol or something?' The Mayor's eyes rolled back into their socket like he had just had a seizure.

'I'm afraid not - decaf coffee?'

'Nah,' barked Jean Marc. 'What was the reason you called then? To tell us we're not on the map. Was that it?'

'No,' said Colin Arthur beaming. 'I wanted to tell you that I've put Crêpe back on the map. If that's any consolation.'

The Mayor looked startled as though waking up from a long dreamless sleep. 'Why didn't you say that in the first place?'

'Sorry, I was leading up to it.'

'What, like a slow heart attack?' Jean Marc joked, slapping the computer geek on the back. 'Are you trying to kill me? Think I prefer you when you were drunk.'

Miss Murs then tapped the super expensive computer screen impatiently with her gigantic wedding ring. 'But why aren't we on here - on this map?'

Colin Arthur inhaled quickly as Miss Murs' ruby nearly went through his screen.

'Let me show you.' He quickly turned the screen towards himself and flicked to a new screen showing The Triangle of Death. 'The previous screen was before I added Crêpe. This one,' he pointed at the screen, 'has Crêpe on it. See.'

'Good God.' Jean Marc gazed at it in disbelief and remembered he felt the same when he saw Jacques for the first time. That feeling of being a father. That impossible sensation a human being only derives from witnessing the birth of his own child. Except this was greater. Here he was actually witnessing the birth of a village. His village. A tiny red dot in cyberspace complete with zero likes, zero reviews, and zero comments.

Colin Arthur saw the Mayor's face. 'I'm sure that will change once people visit, or start searching for your restaurant or Crêperie. Congratulations. You're not lost in the Dark Ages any longer. Also, I've written to IGN asking them to update their records on the road maps. Soon, you'll officially exist everywhere. Not bad after four billion years.' Colin Arthur beamed at them.

'Why four billion years?' asked the Mayor.

'The amount of time the earth has been around.'

'Oh. Really? That long?' he admitted. 'I never knew. No wonder the days sometimes go so slow.' Jean Marc was now sounding more upbeat. After all it was a momentous occasion to be on a map again after four billion years of not being invited to the party. 'Well. Thank you again.'

‘I should be the one thanking you,’ said Colin Arthur. ‘You helped me stop drinking. You made me see sense. And what’s more I’m still trying with Le Glitch so I’ll keep you posted.'

The Mayor's eyes lit up.

'And if I do, you'll be the first to know. In fact, I won't even phone, I'll come by any means available. Promise.'

'I would appreciate that. Coming here gives me the jitters.'

'I was thinking about you the other day when you told me you worked for the post office. Do you remember Minitel?’

‘Yes,’ replied Jean Marc. ‘We had it in the office at the post office, but no one knew how to work it. Most actually thought it was a fax machine.'

‘It wasn’t difficult,’ Colin Arthur declared. ‘Minitel was actually really good, miles ahead of anything the Yanks were doing. But in 1987 a French programmer designed a revolutionary operating system called LoBard which he tried to sell to the French Telegraph Service who designed the Minitel. But here’s the thing, LoBard was better. Only the French government had spent so much money on Minitel that they were not interested in another system. The inventor couldn’t find a backer and LoBard died. Then Minitel became irrelevant when Microsoft and Apple saturated the market with their inferior - in my view - operating systems and here we are today with the same old shit. If we’d had LoBard, computers would start up in seconds and no viruses. Then there was Psion, which in 1989...’

Jean Marc and Miss Murs edged towards the door as Colin Arthur rabbited on.

‘...Anyway, all I want to do now is get my life back together. I even spoke to Caroline the other day and she has dumped that fat restaurant owner from Gigot and is wondering whether she made a mistake. We could all be one happy family again. And really, it's been all down to you and Crêpe. You can have your whisky back as well, it's in the hallway - I won't be needing it.'

'That's great news,' said Jean Marc, already halfway down the hall. 'We'll take the whisky. We might be needing it ourselves.'

And with that they hightailed it out of the house before Colin Arthur started going on about capacitor design in the early 1990s. They then drove back to Crêpe (now officially on the map for the first time in four billion years) via the supermarket, to stock up ready for a long winter of waiting to see if a Scottish boffin from Perth could fix Le Glitch.

Chapter 31 - The Sun

Jean Marc remembered reading in a dense astronomy book when he was a child that in 500 million years the sun would explode and incinerate everything. Everything human beings had ever discovered, written, built, drawn and created would be reduced to ash. Nothing would exist except a few metallic atoms floating around in the vacuum.

Looking out of his kitchen window, Jean Marc understood the author's sentiments. It was being played out in his backyard. In fact, if filmmakers ever wanted a location for a film based on such a premise, they could do worse than come to Crêpe. He should put an ad out in a Hollywood trade mag.

The loneliness and silence of space recreated in rural France. Good rates! Call Jean Marc Bulot (Mayor) on Crêpe 3181

He allowed himself a smile and went to get a glass of wine. Last year at this time he was drinking coffee. That was when he had seen the Ford Galaxy with the Cassidys onboard. He remembered it appearing over the brow of the hill, almost hovering, its wheels cut off by the mirage. That day was hot, he remembered, unseasonably hot, twenty-seven or twenty-eight degrees perhaps.

A lot had happened in a year. More than in any of the previous ten combined. Maybe in his whole life. Some might suggest that at sixty-eight, the mayor, newly married, should simply enjoy his retirement. But he couldn't. Not in the slightest. In fact, he hated it. Last summer had seen the best months of his life. He loved the Glitch and everything it brought with it. Even drunk brattish Brits with their stupid, carefree holiday optimism. Their lack of seriousness and responsibility. Their overbearing sense of entitlement simply because they spoke English.

Not that he didn't like them. He did. When French people went on holiday it wasn't to enjoy themselves, it was to suffer. Things may have changed, but when he went on holiday with his parents, which was rare, and only as far as the Auvergne or the Vosges, it meant listening to his father talk every mealtime, every morning, every afternoon, every evening, even before he went to bed. Then the next day and the next day and the next day until they went home. A holiday for the Bulot family centred on one thing: his father talking. About himself. It was hell.

So when these happy-go-lucky Brits turned up last spring, it warmed him. Holidays should be a time for letting go, not thinking about the year ahead and how difficult it might be, and how they should start economising now, even on holiday. The Brits were really good at this letting-go concept. Eat, drink, fuck, whatever was on offer. Even fifty-centime-a-litre gut churning red wine.

He used to enjoy watching them stagger back to their campers, and then in the morning watch them go for a pee, clutching the sides of their heads like they were having a brain haemorrhage. Fantastic entertainment if nothing else.

That had been the summer. And now, as his astronomy book had predicted, there was silence. Le Glitch had departed. Even Colin Arthur's wizardry in bringing Crêpe back from the dead, hadn't helped in the slightest. He'd even gone to church. Not because of any misplaced guilt; simply because, like the villagers used to do all those years ago, it was something to do.

'Ah Monsieur Mayor,' Le Cure had said. 'Fancy seeing you here.'

'I'm calling in some favours,' Jean Marc replied stoically. 'All those Sunday Schools I went to as a kid. Think I'm owed something.'

A smile crept across the priest's unripe face. 'Come to clear your conscience, Jean Marc?'

'My conscience is fine. How about yours?

The priest smiled again. A docile kind of smile that belongs to people with a highly inflated sense of power. Religious leaders, politicians, football managers, TV celebrities all have it. They smile because they can't think of much else to say. And when they do, all that comes out is a cheap one liner a monkey could have pieced together from discarded Scrabble tiles.

'Confession is free, Jean Marc.'

'I've got nothing to hide. You?'

The priest smiled again and was going to say something else but Jean Marc walked straight past him to see if there was anything to steal.

He and Miss Murs went a few more times but each service failed to inspire them, and confirmed why nobody bothered going any more. Especially when the repeats of Columbo and The Fall Guy invariably clashed with Sunday Mass.

Saying that, even Columbo, his all-time favourite, didn't excite him anymore. Or Miss Murs, who had briefly got addicted to the vague machinations of the rain-jacketed detective. But then got bored. 'It's always the same,' she complained one afternoon. 'You know who did it right from the beginning. The only person who doesn't is Lieutenant Columbo.'

Jean Marc disagreed. 'That's the point, Isabelle. You see the genius of Columbo is that he knows exactly who did it right from the start. His trick is to kid them he's a bumbling halfwit. That way when it comes to the final denouement, the suspects are so utterly bewildered they've been found out, they simply admit their crime and the whole thing is done and dusted within an hour.'

Unfortunately, Colombo's star soon faded in the Bulot household, so much so that they had even discussed moving to Ventrèche. But Miss Murs had vetoed the idea on the grounds that Violette lived there. Not to mention the singular fact that Jean Marc would automatically lose his bet he'd made with Francis over fifty years ago. It was only for a Franc of course, but the thought of losing, and then driving off to Ventrèche with all their stuff piled on top of Madame Coquelicot's Suzuki Ignis, was too much to even consider.

Therefore, they stayed, and not for the first time Jean Marc wished he was like his best friend. So easy for someone like Francis Conda. Warm blankets, TV, stash of wine, four-month supply of cigarettes, tins of confit du canard was his recipe for a blissful winter.

For Jean Marc winter was hell. A nervous animal stuck in a locked room in a locked village in a locked life. Which was why he was so pleased when April spun around again and spring was here. He would get to see his friend again as Francis never missed their annual birthday pissup.

The fifteenth of April, a date as fixed for both of them as Christmas was for Jesus Christ. He was just about to pour another glass and get dressed when he heard something. At first, he thought it was the hum of the microwave 'roasting' another precooked chicken. But then he remembered he'd unplugged the dangerous thing after he'd started getting severe headaches at the top of his cranium. And it wasn't Miss Murs either, who was still asleep after a rather heavy night on the brandy with Ethel Budd.

Plus, the noise seemed to be coming from outside. Probably Bernard. One of the things the old baker had managed to do over the winter was learn to drive. He'd even bought himself a Renault Clio with his savings, to ferry Raymond back and forward every morning and evening to the Lycée in Gigot. He could have gotten the bus like all the other kids but Bernard insisted. After closing down Bar La Boucle (even Francis couldn't prop up a bar on his own - not financially anyway) Bernard's daily drive to Gigot gave him something meaningful to do.

Jean Marc listened and checked the time. Five-thirty. About right as well. Except today was Sunday and even French kids didn't go to school on Sunday. Furthermore, the engine noise was too low pitched for a Renault Clio. A 1.2-cylinder engine revved higher like a hairdryer or a jet washer. This was a heavier sound, bigger cylinders, and yet it sounded strained as though it was struggling with too much weight. It could be the late postal delivery, or the supermarket van, or perhaps Ethel's nephew from England coming to collect her unsold stock.

But something told Jean Marc it wasn't any of these.

He had once read - in a survival guide this time - that if you are out walking in a thunderstorm and the rocks around you start to glow, you're about two seconds from being struck by lightning. He couldn't remember the name of the phenomenon, but he remembered there was a song about it.

This is what he could feel. An energy around him. The air was charged with static. Like the sun exploding. Something big was about to happen.

Chapter 32 - Old Friends

He jumped up and grabbed his new binoculars Miss Murs had bought him for Christmas. They had been intended for bird watching but when he went out in the woods for his first day at his new hobby, he nearly got shot by hunters from Plante, and quickly headed back home to resume his regular position by the window.

'This is it!' he cried out as he focussed his Polar X40 on the inbound vehicle, almost falling out of the window in the process, such was his excitement.

'Miss Murs!' he bellowed as he saw a red coloured GB registered VW California complete with a roof rack full of crap and three bikes hanging off the back like refugees.

'I'm here,' she said standing next to him in her nightgown.

'Oh, you're up. Good. Isabelle. Look, it's a camper. This is it. It's Glitch Day.'

'I can see that.' His wife patted her husband gently on the back like a small ailing dog who'd had a series of seizures and who could barely even pee, let alone breathe. 'But don't get excited dear. You know what happened last week. It could be another false alarm.'

This was true. Last Tuesday a similar camper had turned up, stopped for a few minutes so the driver could relieve himself against one of the plane trees around the square. Then drove off towards Ventrèche.

'Yes I know darling. But we must be ready.'

'You've been saying that all year. And we've seen about eight folk.'

'But it's Glitch Day. My birthday and I've told Madame Coquelicot, Albert, Francis and Bernard to be on standby.'

'But we're all closed up. The restaurant, the Crêperie, the bar. Even Ethel Budd has decided to close her doors.'

'We can open at a moment's notice - I have their word.'

'But Bernard and Francis drank Bar La Boucle dry and I doubt Ethel Budd has got anything left in her shop.'

'She's got some of those hideous pies left over and some flat warm beer. Plus there's always something in Magalie's freezer - it's limitless. There's bound to be something lurking in there.'

'What, like half a horse?'

'I'll pretend I didn't hear that. Come on Isabelle, we'd better go and see who it is. We didn't win the war standing about doing nothing.'

'We didn't win the war,' Miss Murs reminded her husband. 'The Brits and Americans and Russians did. Without them we would be mincemeat in a German Christmas pudding.'

'We'll win this one. Now get dressed. And no more ready meals while I think about it - I'm starting to rot from the inside. And certainly no more microwaving. My brain feels like the inside of Chernobyl.'

After dressing in his standard issue uniform of espadrilles, white silk shirt and blue cloth trousers, Jean Marc raced down the rickety stairs of the Town Hall apartment and outside into the village to greet his latest guests.

'Well if it isn't Alex Cassidy,' cried the Mayor when he saw who it was. 'Great to see you again.'

'You have an excellent memory, Monsieur,'

'Never forget a face,' the Mayor lied. 'But what happened to the old Ford Galaxy?'

'We decided to upgrade,' said Sandra getting out and shaking the Mayor's hand. 'After our experience in Ventrèche in their guesthouse, we decided to buy a camper so we can sleep wherever we want. That guesthouse there was a deathtrap: No fire exits, dirty sheets, and poisonous food. Tim had bed bugs and we got diarrhoea for three days.'

'I'm terribly sorry,' apologised the Mayor.

'I see you haven't got the guesthouse up and running.' Sandra gestured over to the even more derelict looking building.

'Unfortunately not,' apologised the Mayor. 'But we do have a restaurant and a bar and a campsite now. So at least we can provide you with a bite to eat and a place to sleep.'

'What happened?' asked Sandra looking genuinely surprised. 'I mean, last year the village was dead.'

'It's funny you should say that because after you left, we miraculously had a huge influx of visitors.'

'I'm glad.'

'Of course,' said the Mayor looking around. 'This year hasn't got going yet as it's still only April. But we can open our campsite, bar and restaurant in a jiffy.'

'It's a good job we stopped then,' enthused Sandra. 'Because I said to Alex let's go and see that nice Mayor again in Crêpe, see if they've done up that guesthouse.'

'Nothing to do with a dodgy satnav then?' asked Jean Marc a little too quickly.

'Satnav?' questioned Alex. 'Oh no. We had one last year but it broke so we went back to the old-fashioned maps, which was another strange thing because when we looked for

Crêpe, we couldn't find it - luckily we remembered where it was.'

'Ah yes,' said the Mayor. 'They left us off it when they drew them. We're actually famous for it,' the Mayor lied again.

'You should make more of it,' suggested Sandra. 'Advertise it. The lost village or something. The village with no name.'

'Yeh,' scoffed Alex. 'Seeing as you still haven't put that village sign up yet.'

Jean Marc wasn't in the mood for jokes, but smiled anyway.

'Where's this campsite then?' asked Alex. He seemed to be more forceful this year. Less timid.

'Take the road towards Ventrèche then take the first left. End of the road, you can't miss it. It used to be the old stadium.' He was going to launch into the tale about the football match but couldn't be bothered. 'And then when you're ready, come over to the restaurant for dinner. On the house,' insisted the Mayor.

'Oh no,' said Alex.

'Please. Be my guest. It's my birthday.'

'Congratulations!' spouted Sandra, stuffing her Euros back in her pocket as she got back in the car.

As the two adults were discussing something the boy spoke to Jean Marc from the rear window of the camper.

'Looks like the satnav is working properly again,' the boy leered.

'I'm sorry,' replied Jean Marc taken aback by the boy's remark.

The boy leaned in closer to the Mayor. Last year he looked like a little angelic boy fresh out of primary school. A year later he looked positively evil. 'I know what happened last year. Last year the satnav was broken, wasn't it Monsieur

Mayor?' he said mockingly in a voice made for horror films. 'That's why we came here in the first place. That's why you were so busy. But not this year. Look!' he cried out showing the Mayor the screen of his phone.

Jean Marc saw a thick blue line, like a throbbing vein, running straight into Ventrèche along the bypass, Crêpe just a small blip in the middle of nowhere.

'Although,' continued the demonic boy. 'At least you're on the map this year - that's an improvement.'

'You creep!' the Mayor half whispered, half shouted. 'How do you know all this?'

'Because I'm a kid,' he said. 'I know everything.'

'You're behind this, aren't you?' he stammered. 'Le Glitch.'

The boy laughed at him. 'Le Glitch? What are you talking about old man?'

'Le Glitch, you reprogrammed it, didn't you?' The Mayor's eyes darted about frantically.

'Get back on the happy pills Mr. Mayor. You're going to need them seeing as we will probably be the last people you ever see. Ha ha ha ha!'

'Stop bothering the Mayor.' It was Alex. The boy went back to his angelic best.

'Oh no, there's no bother,' said Jean Marc still shaken. He had never known a boy to be so cruel and heartless. Not to mention sinister. Did he know anything, was he behind it, or was he just winding him up? Damn kid. God, in his day, he would've given him a damn good thrashing. Whether the parents were there or not.

'Just having a laugh with your boy. Great humour.'

'What time does the restaurant open?' enquired Alex.

'Six o'clock. But turn up whenever you want. I doubt it will be busy.' Jean Marc looked at the boy in the back who was smiling at him.

Chapter 33 - Jurassic Park

That evening the Cassidys wanted Crêpes. Sandra was vegetarian and both Alex and Tim had eaten so much duck, offal and potatoes over the past few weeks, they were genuinely in need of something light.

But it was not to be. Miss Murs's house speciality was her infamous Crêpe a la Crêpe: a buttery heart-stopping ménage of five Crepes layered in five different cheeses, topped with cream, white wine garlic sauce and grated parmesan. If he'd known, Alex would have gone for a steak.

Jean Marc was glad he didn't though, as it saved him the tedious ordeal of waking Madame Coquelicot up from her winter slumber. Last year the warm weather had brought her out early. But this year with the cold easterly winds, getting her up would be like winding an old carriage clock up that had been kept in a trunk for ninety years with half its innards, cogs and springs hanging out.

If she was even alive that is. He hadn't seen her for weeks. The last time was around Easter when he spied her wandering aimlessly round the square as though walking a dog. And made him wonder if perhaps the perennially playful Madame Coquelicot was finally losing her mind.

The prospect of which caused a pulse of fear to rattle down his spine. Not out of any real sympathy for the woman, after all she was his old teacher, who at school had regularly beaten him with her willow cane. But because the last thing in the world he needed now, especially if Le Glitch did choose to make an appearance, was a dead chef.

Who else would cook? He could microwave a plastic tub of Gratin Dauphinois or boil tins of Confit du Canard, but he couldn't put a meal together. He didn't have that kind of brain. He could sort and post letters, watch cars, memorise names until the end of time. But not cook. Cooking required timing, patience and passion and he had none of these. The ability to bring boiling pots or spitting pans together at the crucial moment to create something far greater than the sum of its individual parts. It was a craft. An art. And despite his enthusiasm and respect for both, he wasn't cut from that cloth. He was a straightforward jobber. A production line worker. Pick, move, drop. Go home.

There was of course Miss Murs. But while she was the absolute queen of Crêpes, by her own admission, she couldn't cook meat. Never had, didn't have a feel for it. All her steaks she had ever cooked for him were either overdone or underdone, never a happy medium. And never medium rare.

As it happened, the only person who could cook to some degree, despite his all eye-and-beard grizzled appearance, was Francis Conda. His regular Sunday banquet for hungry miners in Crêpe's heyday was such a fixture at his house on Rue de Plante, he sometimes had to turn people away. Starting at lunchtime after Mass, it generally lasted till the late hours, with the 'diners' crawling across the village square back to the guesthouse.

He could always recruit Francis and find another barman. But there was a downside to this. Francis' culinary flair was based on one thing. Being drunk, very drunk. Fine when surrounded by other drunks eating the food of a drunk.

A recipe for disaster when cooking for fifty fussy Brits who liked their steaks 'just right'.

It was therefore imperative Madame Coquelicot stayed alive and the Mayor made a note in his office to check on her tomorrow first thing. No one could cook a steak like Madame Coquelicot and no one could cook Crêpes like Miss Murs. It was a winning combination and one he wasn't keen to lose. He would visit her tomorrow, maybe bring her some flowers or some out of date chocolates from Ethel Budd's closed down stock.

Meanwhile, they had the Cassidy's to feed, which went well. Even if Francis had insisted on inviting himself along after throwing his toys out of the pram when Jean Marc informed him they would have to cancel their party.

'But it's our birthday,' he'd complained.

Damn! Jean Marc had forgotten again. Just like last year.

'We have guests, Francis,' he'd informed him. 'I'm sorry, but what do you expect me to do, throw them out on the street, just because it's our big day. We're not married you know.'

'I want to come then. I'll have a table by myself and you can serve me and give me free wine all night.'

Jean Marc agreed, but in the end, Francis joined the Cassidy's that gave them a chance to practice their cranky French. And they loved the food.

'Best food I've had all summer,' congratulated Sandra Cassidy after the first course.

'*Mon plaisir,*' said Miss Murs.

'Me too,' wailed Tim. 'Fantastique!'

'Very rich,' Alex commented wondering if his gym membership was still valid.

Jean Marc was just about to clear away the dishes and serve dessert: Crêpe à la Peche with cream and ice cream, and a bottle of Pineau, when Sandra froze. For a second Jean

Marc thought she might have had a stroke and he might have to call the ambulance or use the defibrillator outside the Town Hall despite the fact no one could remember the access code to unlock the plastic green box.

But then she whispered. 'Shh. What's that sound?'

'What sound?' groaned Alex, his stomach pushing up against his tight nylon shorts.

'Sounds like the dishwasher,' said the boy.

'We don't have a dishwasher,' replied the Mayor who had now joined them at the table.

'Perhaps it's this mysterious Glitch?' giggled Tim mimicking Jean Marc's accent.

'Don't be rude to the Mayor,' scolded Alex.

'But the Mayor wasn't listening. He was looking straight into his wine glass just as he'd done a year ago. Except this time the glass wasn't vibrating. This year there were ripples radiating out from the edge of the glass.

'What are you looking at?' asked Francis.

'Do you remember that first night in the restaurant?'

'Of course, I'll never forget it.'

'Look.' And pointed to the glass.

'It's like Jurassic Park,' commented Alex following their conversation.

Both the old men shook their heads. 'Jurassic Park?'

'It's a bit like Jaws,' offered Alex. 'The film.'

'Yes yes yes,' the two men exclaimed.

'Well instead of a shark, there are dinosaurs. And there's a bit in the film where a T-rex is about to eat them. They know this because there's ripples radiating out from a glass of water and each ripple corresponds to one giant step of the dinosaur.'

They all looked at the glass, all terrified they were about to be eaten by a large predator the size of a house.

'Except here,' Cassidy continued, 'the ripples are distorted and disjointed. As though there's an army of them approaching.

'Holy cow,' said Tim. 'An army of dinosaurs.'

'Or an earthquake,' added Sandra to the list of potential natural disasters about to befall them.

'I can't hear a thing,' replied Miss Murs, annoyed everyone was distracted away from her Crêpe a La Peche.

'Shh everyone,' ordered Jean Marc.

Nobody could deny it any longer. The rumble of engines and the throb of tyres rolling over dry tarmac. Unmistakable and reminded Alex of going to Le Mans as a child with his father: the glow of the brakes at night, the grumble of the cars, and the deafening roar when they came near where they were camping.

'It's Le Glitch,' announced the Mayor.

'What is this damn Glitch?' Sandra demanded.

'It was why we came here last year mum. A glitch in the satnav.'

'Don't be childish Tim,' scolded Sandra. 'This is not a video game.'

'But Mum,' the brat complained. 'Do you remember when the old satnav went bonkers last year and we came here?'

'I thought it was just broken.'

'No. That was Le Glitch. That's why the village has been so busy. Whereas before everyone went straight to Ventrèche missing out Crêpe completely. Look.'

Tim showed everyone his phone. The thick blue line on the screen was now leading straight into the heart of Crêpe.

'It's back!' Jean Marc bellowed grabbing the phone violently from the boy's thin hands. 'This really is it!' the Mayor squealed. 'You're right! It's really happening!'

'It must have clicked in while we were having dinner,' ventured the boy.

'It's incredible!' said Alex. 'Do you mind if I write this down.'

'Write what down?' demanded the Mayor shooting a fierce glare at the Englishman.

'For my book,' Cassidy proclaimed tentatively.

The whole room groaned. The Mayor's head nearly fell into his empty plate, a look of total disgust spreading over his face. Cassidy looked perturbed. He had clearly hit a nerve with the normally placid Mayor.

'What are you going to call it? More Hidden Gems of France.'

'Not sure. But you can be in it if you want?' offered Cassidy.

'Really?' Jean Marc perked up.

'My friend is a publisher.'

'He's not a publisher,' cut in Sandra. 'He writes for the Argos Catalogue.'

'He has contacts,' Alex clarified quickly. 'You never know, you and Crêpe could be famous!'

Vanity overtook frustration immediately at that word 'Famous' as Jean Marc stroked his thick grey hair back with his hand. 'Well, I suppose someone has to record the events here. There was another chap here last year who was writing all of this down, but he went back to England. Maybe he's writing it up as we speak.'

'Could I have first rights?' Cassidy insisted.

'You can have what you want if you write me as a great leader with a glowing character and personality.'

'Anything you want,' said Cassidy producing a notebook from his jacket and writing on the first fresh new page, Le Glitch. 'When did this Glitch start?

'I don't know,' replied the Mayor. 'The day you arrived I suppose. Then it simply vanished on our wedding day last summer and hasn't been seen since. Like a lost dog.'

'And you think it's come back?' asked Cassidy.

'Yes. Unless Colin Arthur fixed it.'

'Who's Colin Arthur?' asked Alex eagerly.

'He's a drunk Scotsman, but he's also happens to be a computer genius who we asked to fix it for us. But let me explain all of this later. Meanwhile, I'll show you what I mean. Come into the square and let's have a look. It might make sense to witness it firsthand. It's quite a scene - it was last year anyway. Like the tanks in 1940.'

'What tanks?' asked Sandra.

'The Nazis!' thundered Jean Marc louder than expected.

Chapter 34 - The Horseman

They were all in the square gazing up the road towards Gigot, marvelling at a thousand pairs of glaring headlights thundering down the road from the bypass, when Sandra Cassidy spotted something else.

'What's that?' She pointed to a figure riding on a horse coming along the road from Ventrèche.

'Jesus, Mary and Joseph,' cried out Miss Murs as though her dead mother had just ridden into town.

Jean Marc looked towards this unholy apparition of a man wearing a kilt and a Hawaiian shirt. Mel Gibson riding into town in a demented remake of Braveheart, a bottle of whisky in one hand, the reins of a horse in the other.

An astonished Alex Cassidy quickly wrote 'The Horseman' in his notebook and underlined it twice.

'Mm, interesting,' mused Tim. 'Enter Colin Arthur.'

'How do you know that?' Alex Cassidy asked his son sternly.

'Who else would it be?' replied the kid. 'Surely this is the mad scientist coming to save the day. Didn't you read comics when you were a kid, Dad?'

Alex Cassidy eyed his son suspiciously. He was only ten but was already showing signs of being cleverer and far more ambitious than his parents. It wasn't difficult seeing as they were both primary school teachers. But it still worried them deeply to see their only child step out of their cloying protective shadow and start developing a personality of his own.

'You're right,' Jean Marc agreed with the boy slapping him on the back, a little too hard for what was probably physically acceptable these days. 'The antihero. The renegade cowboy.'

'The superhero!' the boy whooped with delight.

Jean Marc beamed back at him as he recalled his own childhood. Reading DC and Marvel comics he'd saved up for and bought in Gigot on rare weekends out with his parents. Occasionally getting hold of English copies instead of the lazily translated French editions that repeatedly failed to portray the raging cosmic battles happening across the universe with any real panache.

Alex grunted, crossed out Horseman in his notebook, and wrote down Superhero instead.

'Why is he on a horse?' demanded Sandra.

The boy shrugged nonchalantly. 'Maybe he can't drive?'

Sandra fixed her laser guided glare on her son, then directed it towards the Mayor. The thirty-eight-year-old schoolteacher was not impressed by this anarchic turn of events. Back home in Croydon the most outlandish event that ever happened was people stealing trolleys from the local Waitrose to cart their worldly goods around with them from one hovel to the next. The scene unfolding here was bordering on the Wild West with seemingly no police or authority figure in sight to control things except an unpredictable Mayor and his band of loonies.

'What's going on?' she demanded.

'I don't know,' admitted the Mayor as Colin Arthur galloped up and stopped dead in front of them like a seasoned horseman.

'I've done it,' Colin Arthur screamed. 'I've got the Glitch back. I told you I would come and tell you Monsieur Mayor. I promised, didn't I?'

'On a horse?' Jean Marc was eyeing the bottle.

'Yes, I stole it from Monsieur Arnold. Figured it was the only way to get here with all this traffic, plus I can't get busted for being drunk on a horse, can I?'

'I thought you were on the wagon?'

Colin Arthur shook his head. 'Caroline left me again so I fell off it.'

'Well thank you anyway for fixing *Le Glitch*,' offered Jean Marc belatedly. 'But to be honest. I think I'd figured that out already.' He pointed to the mass of cars and vehicles coming over the brow of the hill.

'Christ,' proclaimed Colin Arthur.

'Is everything OK?' asked the Mayor.

'I think so.' Colin Arthur looked unsure.

'What do you mean, you think so,'

'Do you remember *Le Glitch* last year?'

The Mayor nodded.

'Well imagine this as the child of *Le Glitch*. A big bouncing baby *Le Glitch* if you like. Or *Le Glitch Plus*. Or *Le Glitch* version 2.0. An upgrade.'

'Why are you worried?'

'No no no, I'm not,' exclaimed the computer boffin. 'I'm ecstatic. It's just a little bit of a shock that's all to see it in person. You know I've worked all winter on this and now to finally see it in action is quite satisfying.'

What Colin Arthur had failed to mention was that the entire village probably had about three minutes left before the US 4th Fleet based in the Med sent over a couple of Tomahawk missiles to totally wipe them out. He wasn't sure whether shifting satellites was regarded as terrorism these days. But seeing as tiny villages in Yemen were being razed to the ground for tuning into the World Service on Iranian made transistors, he wasn't going to chance it. And having noted that every other route was blocked, he realised his only viable escape route lay in the fields and hedgerows beyond the village. Hence the horse.

'This is incredible,' remarked Alex Cassidy to his wife. 'Look, I've already got down a list of characters.' He showed her his notebook like a small child showing mummy his homework.

Sandra looked at it impassively. 'I couldn't care less to be honest.'

'Someone has to write this down,' insisted Alex.

'Why?' exploded Sandra hopping up and down. 'What's so special about it? It's just a traffic jam. It happens in Croydon all the time. Haven't you noticed?'

'This isn't Croydon, Sandra. It's a small deserted village in the middle of nowhere. They don't normally have traffic jams here. They don't even have traffic. Don't you want to know what's happening? Because I do.'

He stubbed his pen into a spot on his notebook making a splattered dot. Maybe in years to come when he was a famous writer, that dot would signify the beginning, his precious notebook sold for a million pounds in an auction long after he was dead.

'I don't want to read about a traffic jam, Alex; there's plenty where we live thank you very much,' blazed Sandra.

'Who are you anyway?' The Scotsman looked suspiciously at the Englishwoman.

'I'm his mother.' She pointed at the boy. 'And the wife of him.' She jabbed a pointy finger at Alex. 'And you're drunk and clearly mad.' She looked up at the horseman. 'And now we're leaving.'

She looked at Jean Marc. 'Sorry Monsieur Mayor and thank you for a lovely dinner, but where I come from, this simply doesn't happen.'

Jean Marc and Miss Murs were about to add that where they came from, it didn't happen either. But the angry teacher cut them off.

'Alex! Tim!' barked Sandra.

'Aww,' complained the boy almost crying.

'You go along, Sand,' suggested Alex. 'We'll catch you later.'

'What!' Her face went as red as autumn cherries. 'What do you mean, you'll catch me later? What do you think I am, a bus? If you feel that way, you can make your own way home. Write your precious novel from the gutter, see if I care. And it's Sandra. Not Sand.'

'Just give us ten minutes, Sandra,' pleaded Cassidy. 'This man on the horse is just about to explain what's happening.'

'I'm leaving,' said Sandra emphatically and grabbed Tim. But he wasn't going to miss this for the world and quickly broke free and rushed back to stand by his father. Leaving Sandra Cassidy to head off towards the camper on her own, looking, if everyone was perfectly honest, a little bit stupid.

'I'll phone you later then,' said Alex.

'I wouldn't worry about her,' advised Colin Arthur. 'She won't get far.

'Why not?' asked Cassidy.

'That's what I'm about to explain.'

Chapter 35 - Don Quixote

Colin Arthur was about to launch into his explanation, when they all saw another figure charging down the road from Ventrèche. But the figure wasn't on a horse - it was on a bicycle.

'And I thought I'd seen everything,' declared the Mayor when he saw Michel Arnold pedalling down the road in cowboy boots, a pair of faded denim jeans, a 1970s wide collar shirt and a string tie.

'All we need now is his wife,' the Scotsman joked.

A second later Violette rode into town on an ancient Peugeot racer dressed in a spandex boobtube four sizes too small for her and a pair of luminous leggings. An incredible sight, swooned Jean Marc, mainly because in all the years he'd known her, she had never once shown any interest in sports or cycling whatsoever. Now she was careering into the village like a demented reincarnation of Eddie Merckx.

'Sancho Panza, I suppose,' mumbled Tim.

'Who?' Alex questioned his son.

'Sancho Panza: the original sidekick,' repeated Tim. 'You know, Don Quixote.'

Alex Cassidy's mind was churning very slowly. 'I've never heard of him. Did he play for Barcelona?'

His son closed his eyes and let the sunshine permeate through his eyelids for a few seconds. It was quite clear that his so-called educated teacher dad was actually quite stupid. Three years of university, another year studying to be a teacher, then another year gaining an MA (in teaching) had reduced his IQ to single figures, maybe even zero, if that was possible. It was embarrassing, and worse of all, he had a whole eight years left before he could leave home. Then he would ditch education all together and seek his knowledge elsewhere. Like a cave in Borneo.

'No Dad,' Tim groaned deciding not to embarrass his father any further. 'I think that was Lionel Messi. Don Quixote played for Real Madrid.'

'Ah, of course, how stupid of me,' Alex Cassidy congratulated himself just as the two Tour de France contenders arrived triumphantly in the village square. A square that now held a crowd of around fifty, who had gathered thinking some impromptu theatre was being put on by the local village troupe. Costumes, horses and all.

'Good evening,' coughed Michel Arnold puffing and spluttering like the train that used to run from Gigot to Crêpe and Ventrèche before it was shut down.

'Not quite the athlete we once were, eh?' gaffed Jean Marc unable to resist a dig.

'I'll thrash you at any game known to mankind Jean Marc Bulot. Just name it,' challenged Michel, his chest pumping up and down like a small mammal.

'Draughts? You might just manage a game without needing an oxygen mask to breathe through.'

'I'm in perfect physical health.' He coughed up a ball of black tarry phlegm just as Violette pulled up, gasping over the handlebars.

'Hi Violette,' welcomed Jean Marc. 'What's your role in this pantomime?'

'I'm following him,' she looked at Michel.

'Why?' asked Jean Marc.

‘Ask him.’ Michel pointed to Colin Arthur.

‘Although,’ Violette suggested. ‘Maybe we should tell our bit first. Then everything might be in the correct sequence.’

‘OK. Go on then,’ conceded Jean Marc warily, wondering how it had all come down to this, and desperately regretting letting go of those dreamy days of looking aimlessly out of the kitchen window.

'So,' started the Mayor of Ventrèche. 'We were both enjoying our meal when we saw an orange camper.'

'The Young Couple,' yelled Miss Murs excitedly. She had now been joined by Albert, Francis and Bernard to complete the original cast of this absurd soap opera unfolding in a small village in the middle of France.

'The who?' sighed Michel, angry he had been interrupted after only one line.

'A young couple from England who came here last year,’ added Albert. ‘But they left in November as they were slowly going insane. But maybe they’ve picked up Le Glitch again and come back.’

‘Well they didn't get far,’ cried Michel Arnold, impatient to get on with his story. ‘Because suddenly there were hundreds of them. All nationalities, not just French. British, German, Swiss, Spanish, Italian, Dutch. It didn't make sense. So we flagged one down.'

‘What happened?’ drooled Alex Cassidy scribbling like a madman.

‘Well, incredibly, the guy we asked said he was on a business trip to Marseille when for some unknown reason his satnav redirected him to Crêpe. I didn’t believe him so I asked some others and they all told me a similar story. They were from all over - it was like the bloody wacky races. There was even a Swiss couple who were on their way to Austria. You should have seen their faces when I told them they were about a thousand kilometres off course.'

Everyone laughed.

‘It was funny I admit, but it didn't make any sense,’ continued Michel. ‘They kept on coming, so I ordered the Gendarmes to block the roads. Then I saw Colin Arthur here galloping down the road on my horse and decided to follow him.’

‘On bicycles?’ questioned Francis looking at the two Peugeot racers.

Michel Arnold looked down at his Peugeot. ‘I couldn’t get my Buick out of the garage because the roads were blocked so we had to use our bicycles. It’s a bit of a mess really.’ He looked up towards Colin Arthur but only got as far as the horse's backside, his neck cricked from riding his bicycle for the first time in twenty years. 'Why are you on my horse anyway?'

Colin Arthur looked down at the animal’s head perhaps forgetting in all the commotion, not to mention the fact he was totally pissed, that he was actually on a horse.

‘It was the only transport I could find to get here,’ replied Colin Arthur. 'Seeing as the road was blocked and there was all this traffic.'

That seemed to satisfy Michel. Under normal circumstances he would probably call for his arrest, but this wasn't normal. 'Can you put him back when you've finished,’ he remarked as though Colin Arthur had borrowed a brush.

'Fine,' agreed the drunk waving his hand in the air.

'But perhaps, you'd like to finish your story first.'

‘Long or short version?' The Scotsman asked.

‘Short!' everyone cried out.

'OK,' he started. 'After I'd put Crêpe back on the map, the next thing I needed to do was nudge one of the satellites in order to send all the traffic back through the village as it did before. But to do this, I had to alter the atomic clocks onboard one of the satellites by about 4/5ths of a millionth of a nanosecond.'

'Wow,' exclaimed Cassidy, pen in hand. 'How long is 4/5ths of a millionth of a nanosecond, I mean roughly?'

Colin Arthur's mind sprang into action, his brain now processing information faster than the whole village combined. And this was despite having drunk nearly two bottles of malt whisky over the course of the day.

'Think of those super slow-motion replays of penalty appeals in football matches where the player goes to ground theatrically after tripping over his opponent's boot laces. Can you picture that?'

Alex Cassidy nodded. An image of Lionel Messi flying through the air after a fierce tackle from Don Quixote flashed through his mind. 'Yes, I can, quite clearly in fact.'

'Good. Now imagine that same replay slowed down about eight million times. The player suspended in midair, hanging in space for eternity. But he's not. He's still moving, just incredibly slowly. It's just that our eyes can't detect it because the time interval in between each frame of film is too small. A time interval that roughly works out at about 4/5ths of a millionth of a nanosecond.'

Colin Arthur looked down at Cassidy from his horse. 'Does that answer your question?'

Cassidy stared back at him. 'Err, yes, I think so,' replied the confounded teacher doodling something in his notebook that looked like a kite.

'He means it's very small, Dad,' Tim impatiently informed his father. 'Almost nothing.'

'Exactly!' commended Colin Arthur excitedly. 'And taking this idea a step further young man. Due to this extreme time compression, if you actually sat down to watch the player hit the turf, roll around in unmistakable agony for a few minutes, then wait for the referee's decision as to whether it was a penalty or not, life on Earth would have ceased to exist long ago. In fact, by the time you eased your fat arse out of your La-Z-Boy armchair and wandered outside to put your empty six-pack in the trashcan, all you would see in front of you was a baked desert where once there was a country called France.'

Nobody said anything. Because nobody, except possibly Tim, had a clue what he was talking about. Either Colin Arthur's mind was as frazzled as the crazed apocalyptic visions in his head. Or he was simply on a different plane to everyone else.

Jean Marc was about to ask whether this theory had anything to do with exploding suns, but Michel Arnold spoke first.

'Sorry to interrupt your science lesson Monsieur Arthur,' the Mayor of Ventrèche cut in facetiously. Still unable to raise his head any higher, he now found himself eyeballing the horse's testicles. 'I mean this is all very interesting, but I'd like to clear something up first.'

'Of course,' replied Colin Arthur cheerfully, thinking he was about to be quizzed further on his idea.

'You said you were trying to get this Glitch back for Crêpe. That implies you were working for them. Is this true?'

'Oh. Well, yes,' admitted Colin Arthur. 'But I was only trying to help.'

Why?' demanded Michel sternly. 'You live in Ventrèche. You owe these people nothing.'

'They paid me.'

'No, we didn't you liar,' countered Miss Murs angrily.

'You paid me in whisky, remember?' He held the bottle up as though to prove it.

Michel Arnold turned to face Miss Murs, then Jean Marc. 'So, this is what's been happening, I get it now. That's why you were mooning around Ventrèche last year.'

‘We were just trying to protect our livelihood,’ insisted the village secretary.

‘This doesn't concern you Miss Murs,’ ordered Michel brusquely.

‘How dare you speak to my wife like that,’ thundered Jean Marc. ‘And it’s Mrs. Bulot to you, you jumped up cowboy.

‘You bastard!’ bawled Michel Arnold launching himself towards his opposite number. Although it wasn’t really a launch, more a half-aimed lurch forward. ‘I’ve always hated you, you tall pompous bastard.’

‘Get off, you silly man,’ roared Jean Marc as he grappled Michel Arnold to the ground and threw him to the floor in an expert judo roll.

‘You’re in Crêpe now,’ he screamed into the face of his opposing number.

'And if you try that again or speak to my wife like that, I’ll hang you from the hooks in the Town Hall. They haven’t been used for a while, but I’m sure they’ll take your weight. Although then again I’m not sure.’

Jean Marc was just about chop him in the solar plexus which would have probably killed him when he stopped. This wasn’t a time for violence. They had a crisis on their hands. He looked at Michel struggling for air on the floor. Violette was crying. Miss Murs wasn’t.

‘Come on Michel,’ said Jean Marc with an air of a great leader. ‘Let’s not fight, we have things to do.’

‘I wanted to make up last year but you wouldn’t have it,’ spluttered Arnold.

‘Well I’m ready now.’

‘Can I get up and we can listen to the rest of Colin Arthur's story, it was just getting interesting.’

Jean Marc had his knee on Arnold’s neck. ‘OK. But one last thing.’ A smile spread across Jean Marc’s face, as he realised, especially after listening to Colin Arthur's fantasy about diving footballers, that this was the opportunity he'd been waiting for since 1967. 'I want to talk about football.'

'What now?' said an astonished Michel Arnold. 'Hardly the time, but I think Marseille won 2-0 earlier. Think they were playing Guingamp. Straight forward win. Goals either side of half time. Or are you supporting PSG now like everyone else?'

'No, you clown. The Crêpe-Ventrèche match.'

'The Cup Final?'

'Yes. The 1967 Cup Final.' The Mayor said it like it was the 1970 World Cup Final. 'I want to know what happened.'

Chapter 36 - The 1967 Cup Final

Jean Marc still had his knee firmly on Michel Arnold's neck. A lot of water had passed under the bridge since that violent day over fifty years ago. The ebb and flow of life in this drab part of Gigot County had brought them little except a couple of broken marriages, three estranged boys and two dull careers. And now the humdrum trickle of their existence had brought them back to where it had all started. Jean Marc Bulot and Michel Arnold, the two opposing captains from the 1967 Gigot County Cup Final, fighting it out once again on the streets of Crêpe.

'I can't hear you, Arnold,' growled Jean Marc, increasing the pressure with almost demonic pleasure.

'Can you get off my neck?' winced Arnold.

'Sorry? What was that?'

'Right! Stop this nonsense, Jean Marc.' It was Violette. 'You're going to break his neck.'

'So?' said Jean Marc grinning down at his old adversary who was twitching like an animal who'd just been run over by a car.

'Stop it!' she cried.

'It's only a bit of horseplay, Violette,' he countered, giving him a firm thump in the kidneys with his other knee. 'He's fine, aren't you Michel?'

‘Yesss,’ whimpered the Mayor of Ventrèche still trying to play the hard man.

‘Go on then,’ relented Jean Marc. ‘Stand up if you can, tell us what happened. Was the match fixed or not? We’re all waiting.’

Michel Arnold got to his feet, pulled his lapels tight, fixed his string tie, straightened out his shirt and started talking.

‘Yes, Jean Marc. The match was fixed. There, I’ve said it. Satisfied?’

‘Is that it? You make it sound so normal. Almost inconsequential.’

'What else do you want? A written bloody confession. It's the way it is. Everything around here is fixed. Everything is crooked. Always has been. Always will be. How do you think all these tiny villages survive, hmm? Waiting for Paris to throw us a few quid. Ha! Why should we watch all the posh villages with their fancy festivals and fireworks prosper while we scrape around in the mud? There are 36,000 villages in this blasted country. Do you think all of them feature in films with Johnny Depp? Or have art galleries and cheese evenings and concerts and jazz?'

‘Plante has a jazz festival,’ Jean Marc reminded him.

‘Plante doesn’t have a jazz festival,’ exclaimed Michel.

‘Francis said it does.’

‘It doesn’t,’ clarified Francis. ‘I’ve told you before Jean Marc. It’s just a few friends of that mad doctor from Ireland who put up a stage made of wooden pallets, get incredibly drunk and play endless blues until dawn. Then they eat bacon and eggs and doughnuts and go to bed until three in the afternoon, then get up and do it all again. That’s not a jazz festival, that’s a bender.’

‘Well it doesn’t mean we’re all crooks,’ continued Jean Marc. ‘Just because we don’t have a bloody jazz festival or fireworks.’

'Come on Jean Marc,' Michel Arnold blared. 'Think about it! Without this mysterious Glitch you would be sinking into the mud like the rest of us.'

'*Le Glitch*,' Jean Marc corrected him rather pedantically considering the delicate state of proceedings.

'Whatever, Jean Marc,' Michel fumed. 'The point is, Crêpe is no different from anywhere else. We all have to take what we can get, otherwise we die. Just like every other small community in the entire world. There's simply not enough cash to go round. Cities and big towns always get the best treatment because that's where most people live, which is where the votes are. Politicians only give a toss about the countryside when the farmers go on strike or start throwing shit into the roads. Then they throw them a bit of cash and hope they'll drink themselves to death or better still hang themselves. Come on Jean Marc, you've lived here all your life, you know what the deal is.'

'He's right.' It was Miss Murs.

'What!' Jean Marc exploded. 'What on earth are you talking about Miss Murs?'

'Michel Arnold is right,' she declared.

'I can't believe I'm hearing this.' He said with a disdainful tone, almost chilling.

'Because he's telling the truth,' she reinforced bravely. 'None of us have paid a cent in taxes. A dime in social security. Or a nickel in employee healthcare contributions, or training or safety.'

She wasn't sure why she was using American slang, maybe because she'd spent the entire winter watching American cop shows. Or perhaps because it sounded more catchy. 'Because if we had done that, we would have given all our money away to be spent on TGV networks miles away from here. Networks whose only real purpose is to increase local property prices when people realise they can commute to Paris in only two hours from a cow shed in the Pyrenees which has been converted into a Yoga studio. That's why we keep our money here!' She pointed to the ground.

'Bravo!' cried Michel and started applauding. 'Great speech Miss Murs. You should come and work for us.'

'Watch it Michel,' boomed Jean Marc squaring up to his rival again. 'But anyway, what's all this got to do with the football match?'

'Because Ventrèche was poor at the time. Crêpe had just discovered coal. Whereas we had nothing except a rundown flour mill that produced poor grade flour half of which was grit. My father, who was Mayor, couldn't face watching Crêpe win the County Cup, so he had a word with the referee, who happened to be the uncle of Jacques Breton.

He was a postman as well and did reffing at the weekends. Except he had a penchant for gambling and so a few extra Francs from my father persuaded him to throw the match. If we were losing Jacques would go down in the area and the ref would award a penalty. The rest you know.'

'So we went through all of that just so your dad could feel better about himself.' Jean Marc genuinely looked astonished. 'Why didn't he simply get drunk like everyone else? Or go with a prostitute – Christ, I'd have paid for it if I'd known.'

Michel smirked at the thought of his rickety old father entertaining a prostitute from the rough end of Gigot, then promptly wiped it from his mind. 'He probably didn't think it was a big deal at the time.'

'It was a big deal to me!' Jean Marc barked. 'It practically ruined my life.'

'I'm sorry,' admitted Michel. 'I didn't know it would create so much bad feeling.'

'But look at all the mess it made. The riots. We both got banned for a year and the stadium was wrecked - still is.'

'I think there would have been a riot anyway. There was a lot of anger going around. Just an excuse for a fight really.'

'Do you know how many years it took me to get over that Michel?'

'No.'

'Fifty.'

'Really?'

'In fact, until this summer, I've thought about Jacques Breton's dive every morning.'

'Footballers dive all the time,' offered Michel. 'It's part of the game. Even back in the 1960s.'

'Yes. But generally, they don't wreck my life. It might wreck your evening if your team loses because some Portuguese falls over in the box in the last minute. But it doesn't destroy your entire life.'

'You were always so melodramatic Bulot,' insisted Michel.

Murmurs of agreement all round.

'I'm sorry anyway.' Michel offered his hand.

The tension in the crowd was palpable.

Jean Marc looked at his opposite number.

Maybe it was time. Maybe this was the moment he'd been waiting for all his life in front of all these people. On the shiny limestone slabs he'd laid all those years ago. The same slabs that had cost €39,000 and got him a firm reprimand from the Prefecture for a wilful waste of village resources on a square no one ever used.

'Maybe you're right,' he said.

Then rather awkwardly as though he was reaching out to touch a prickly cactus, shook Michel Arnold's hand to a hearty round of applause.

'And the ref?' asked Jean Marc hoping to conclude the whole sorry affair. 'What happened to him? Suppose he gambled all his money away and died a horrible lonely death on the side of the road in Montluçon or some such hellhole?'

Michel looked sheepish. 'Not quite.'

The audience sensed a denouement.

'I hate to say this but he became La Poste's Regional Director for Gigot County. He was the one responsible for closing you down. He was the one who made the final decision.'

'Alain Gilbert! He was the match ref.'

Michel Arnold nodded.

'Hang the ref,' someone shouted.

'Well I'm going to make sure he's arrested and prosecuted, and his pension stripped,' railed Jean Marc. 'I can't believe he got away with it.'

'I think you might have a job there.'

'Why? Has he covered it up, made someone sign something so he has complete immunity?'

'Not really. He's dead.'

'Hooray,' came a chorus of cheers.

'He died in Biarritz as it happened. On holiday.'

Jean Marc cracked an ironic smile. 'Oh well. Can't say I'm sorry.'

'No, neither am I,' echoed Michel Arnold. 'He was my boss, a real petty-minded moron.'

Jean Marc looked up at Michel Arnold. 'I suppose we're all square then?'

'I guess so.'

'But I want the trophy,' Jean Marc suddenly demanded stamping his foot on the limestone slabs.

That stunned the crowd. They didn't expect such a childish tantrum at this stage in the proceedings. They thought Jean Marc might make a graceful exit. But clearly the man was more of a baby than they thought.

'Why don't we call it a draw?' suggested the Mayor of Ventrèche. 'We'll say the match was tied at 2-2 - I'll even amend it in the official records in our Town Hall.'

'I want the trophy,' Jean Marc insisted.

'You can have it,' agreed Michel Arnold. 'It's cluttering up my office anyway.'

Jean Marc turned to face Michel Arnold again, ready for round two.

'Get him! Duff him up!' shouted someone.

'I think this is enough,' yelled Miss Murs now totally fed up with the two mayors. 'Colin Arthur,' she went on turning to the Horseman. 'Will you please carry on with your story.'

There was a large murmur of agreement.

'Excuse me,' some timid man asked, clutching himself like a small boy. 'Could we take a wee break, come back in say ten, fifteen minutes?'

'No!' snapped Miss Murs glaring at the man. 'This is real-life theatre; you'll have to suffer for a bit longer until it's over. Now, Monsieur Arthur, please continue.'

'Yes,' replied Colin Arthur. 'Where was I?'

'You were talking about slow motion falling footballers and altering clocks onboard satellites,' someone in the crowd reminded him.

'Ah yes. Thank you. So, I'd managed to change the time alright - 4/5th of a millionth of a nanosecond.' He paused. 'Except I got the wrong satellite. I mean, it's complicated, there's hundreds of these things flying around the earth and the numbers are so similar. RGFT 5555-7774TYH or RGFT 5555-7774TYJ. Crazy! You'd think they would give them recognizable names like we give to pets. Here comes Rover. Here comes Fido. Here comes Pluto. So in a moment of haste, I configured RGFT 5555-7774TYP instead of RGFT 5555-7774TYQ. Sobriety you see. You start taking things for granted, you're moving too fast. When you're drunk, you slow down, you take care, everything is done at a slower rate, less room for mistakes.'

'Meaning?' asked Jean Marc impatiently.

'Meaning, I nudged the wrong satellite.'

'Meaning?' Jean Marc reiterated.

'Meaning, there's going to be quite a lot of vehicles arriving quite soon.'

'There's quite a lot here already, if you hadn't noticed.'

'Think more, then double it. Triple it in fact.'

'How many more?' demanded the Mayor.

'A lot more.'

'Can't you be more precise?' Jean Marc was starting to unravel; he could feel it in his heart and his head. A manic pumping from one organ to the next as though he had been turned up to full power.

'At this point, no,' admitted Colin Arthur.

'You're useless! God! And I thought you were a genius. But no! I'm surrounded by idiots. Why can't someone give me a straight answer? Like why are all these people here, and where are they from?' demanded Jean Marc, a cloud of dust the size of an atomic bomb billowing up behind the village as the cars and vehicles kept on piling into Crêpe.

'I agree.' Now it was Michel Arnold's turn to display some authority. 'If you don't tell us what's going on Monsieur Arthur. The Mayor of Crêpe and I will make a joint arrest for wasting public time. And stealing my horse.'

'Oh fucking Christ!' Colin Arthur yelled. 'I'm so fucking scared. What are you going to do? Stop my baguette order at the fucking boulangerie, is that what you do round here? Cancel our daily bread?'

'If we have to, yes,' said both the men, who were actually serious.

‘Please shut up you two,’ cried Colin Arthur. ‘I mean honestly, have you ever seen two such silly men in all your life?’

That seemed to garner wide agreement from the crowd.

‘You’ve got cars from all over Europe chugging up your roads and yet you still can’t put two and two together to figure out what’s happening. Do you need it drawn in big coloured letters?’

‘Yes,’ accepted Michel Arnold.

‘Fuck you then! I’ll let your secretary spell it out for you on an Etch-A-Sketch, then afterwards you can go and play with your tea sets. Because I’m sorry gentlemen but it’s time for me to leave. Goodbye. Or should I say *Au Revoir*!’

He then pulled on the reins and galloped off into the sunset across the green clover-filled fields of Gigot County. Just as Paulo the Thief had done with Madame Lafarge's handbag under his arm almost thirty years earlier.

Michel Arnold thought about chasing him but he was on a bicycle. Jean Marc also thought about it. But he was too late, as normal.

Chapter 37 - History

As it happened, the two mayors' chronic indecision wouldn't have changed Crêpe's place in history. While they stood arguing once again about what to do, a traffic jam, later described by the UN as the longest traffic jam in history, was forming behind Crêpe. An 839 kilometre long *Bouchon* that gridlocked most of France and parts of Switzerland and Italy for a fortnight. It took a team of CIA engineers an entire month to untangle Colin Arthur's handiwork, and reposition the offending satellite, RGFT 5555-7774TYP.

And even after they'd finished, they still weren't really sure if it was functioning properly, and had considered casting it adrift into deep space where it could do no more damage. Then sending Colin Arthur the bill - if they could ever find him.

What was not up for debate was that Crêpe, after years of being cast adrift from Planet Earth and The Universe as a whole, was most definitely now on the map.

Hours after Colin Arthur had made his bid for freedom, newscasters and journalists from all over the world were descending on this tiny village in the middle of nowhere. Photos, diagrams and news copy flowed from Crêpe like it was a war zone. The *Place de Crêpe* and *Camping Crêpe* became nerve centres for the entire Western news machine, with presenters, technical staff and supplies having to be helicoptered in such was the gridlock.

One battle hardened war correspondent from the BBC, who had been holidaying nearby, described it as one of the most chaotic situations he had ever seen.

'It's literally a disaster zone,' he reported. 'Cars and vehicles and families everywhere looking for something to eat. Fights and riots breaking out, even among the Mayor and officials, and with more heavy traffic on the way I can only see the situation worsening.'

When *Le Glitch* was finally corrected and the traffic and the people and the reporters and journalists were gone, Crêpe became like any other village that had had a brief moment of fame. It ruthlessly mined and milked it for all it was worth.

Le Restaurant, La Crêperie, Bar La Boucle and Ethel Budd's Shop made a steady income off the back of *Le Glitch*. A giant bronze plaque was erected (at huge expense) in the village square to commemorate the event and mark the spot where the longest traffic jam in history started. Francis, Albert, Bernard, Madame Coquelicot, Ethel Budd, Miss Murs, and Raymond continued to make good livings. And Jean Marc was permanently installed as Mayor, receiving a medal in the post from Le President himself.

'An ironic gesture,' Le President cited in his press release, 'seeing as Monsieur Bulot was once a postman - the heart and soul of our glorious Republique.'

Alex Cassidy wrote a book on it called The Longest Traffic Jam in History that further cemented Crêpe's place on the map. It was later adapted into a film and made Alex Cassidy relativity famous, much to the consternation of the Young Man who claimed it was his idea and that Cassidy had hijacked it. A claim also put forward by that pompous arse Henry Clark, who argued he was the first person 'to discover'

Crêpe and so he should have the right to write the story. He took Cassidy to court where he lost and had to sell his Land Rover to cover the costs. The judge threw the case out on the grounds that it was no one's idea: *Le Glitch* just happened and Alex Cassidy was the first to write it down. Case dismissed!

Although saying that, not everything that was written was totally true. Madame Coquelicot's ten years in Paris were portrayed in the book and the film as debauched and wild. Living as a translator by day and a dancer by night in a whirlwind of romance, illicit drugs, alcohol and sex. In reality, it was nothing of the sort.

When Cassidy had interviewed her for the book, she blatantly made it all up. She hadn't meant to at all. It just came out. The life she might have lived if things had been different. The life everyone thought she had lived because she had never denied it.

Her real life was slightly different. After finishing her studies and finding herself totally broke, she got a job in a travel agent. There she spent ten years booking tickets to exotic places for rich folk while living alone in a small flat near Montparnasse. She enjoyed reading, going to the cinema and the occasional dance. There were a few flings but nothing more. Then one day she felt homesick and went home to Crêpe. A year later she married Cyrille who had taken over her parents' butcher's shop, had no children and lived a fairly dull life teaching idiots like Francis, Jean Marc and Violette.

But what the hell. At ninety-two she was too old for the truth and gave everyone what they wanted. Which was that for ten years Madame Coquelicot had lived a crazy life in Paris. And it worked, the film was a hit, and everyone loved it. In fact, she was so convinced by the performance, she almost believed it herself. Why not? Everyone else did.

Cassidy went on to write another book called *Le Piste* based on almost identical events to *Le Glitch*. But instead of a village in the middle of nowhere, it was based in a ski lodge in the Alps. It flopped and Cassidy went back to teaching. Eventually doing a Ph.D in it, much to the dismay of Tim who heard about this from his cave in Borneo.

But all of this happened much later.

Back to 15th April 2019 and this village pantomime wasn't quite over. The crowd was watching Colin Arthur ride across the fields of Gigot County, when who should amble down the main road, but the Queen of Sin herself, Madame Coquelicot.

'Ah,' cried the Mayor to the old woman. 'Am I glad to see you.'

'What on earth is going on Bulot?' she cried bringing up her hand to her mouth and nose to protect her from the ever-increasing smog. 'Do you know I was in such a lovely sleep until I was awoken by this racket.'

'We've really no time to explain. We need to feed everybody. And quickly.'

'I'm not feeding all of these people - I'm not Jesus Christ. Plus, I've got nothing left except a few ends of horse...'

The village fell silent.

The air thinned.

The temperature plummeted.

Even the sound of a coin dropped by a small child over three kilometres away could be head reverberating round the village square like a cymbal.

'Shit,' groaned Jean Marc seeing his moment of glory slip away. Everything he had ever hoped for had been dashed by one careless slip of the tongue from his onetime teacher. 'Brilliant,' he cursed. 'Fucking brilliant!'

'Did she say horse?' someone from the crowd murmured.

'Yeah,' another man said. 'You're not eating horse, are you?'

'We love horses.'

'Murderers!'

The crowd was restless. Tension rising. He could feel the energy and knew he had about two seconds to rescue everything he had ever tried to achieve in his silly life. If not, it would be washed away down the toilet like everything else.

But he couldn't think of anything. There was no escape plan available and as the crowd came for him like zombies, he knew life had finally beaten him. He was done.

'Pies, anyone?' came a voice.

The crowds retreated as Ethel Budd entered the limestone square carrying a tray of steaming meat pies.

'Wow!' came hungry voices.

'That's just the ticket.'

'Fray Bentos pies. I haven't had one of those for years.'

'Me, neither.'

The audience was drooling. Even the European contingent who had never heard of Fray Bentos pies looked hungry. Even the Swiss.

No one was thinking anymore of horses. Jean Marc had been saved by the bell. Thank God for Miss Budd.

'Ladies and gentlemen,' he announced. 'If you would like to make your way over to the restaurant, we'll bring the pies over. And free beer as well!'

A roar went up and everyone started rushing over.

'Excuse me. Is there a vegetarian option?' some irritating person then asked.

Sandra Cassidy of course, who else? Somehow, she had managed to worm her way back into the crowd from God only knows where.

'Sandra,' Miss Murs exclaimed politely. 'How about a Crêpe?'

'Yes please,' said the thirty-eight-year-old teacher.

'Everyone,' belted out Miss Murs determined to have the last line in this absurd melodrama. 'As well as pies, we'll also be serving Crêpes in La Crêperie in half an hour. And by the way. Welcome to Crêpe.'

Everyone started applauding. The performance had finally finished.

Even Colin Arthur heard the clapping as he galloped aimlessly across Gigot County.

'That must be for me,' he cried out taking a final swig of whisky before tossing the empty bottle in a hedge. Then he smiled, punched the air a few times, and rode off into the sunset, never to be seen again.

Author's Note

While Crêpe and Ventrèche are clearly fictional and their location kept vague, the events described in this novel could have happened anywhere in France.

And may do in the future...

Acknowledgements

I'm greatly indebted to the following for help with this novel. Elizabeth for the time-consuming job of reading my many manuscripts, not to mention the constant support, love and chocolate cake. Peggy Milligan for proofreading. Justin P Brown for design advice. Members of the Caussade Cyclo Club for cultural tips. The Prefecture in Montauban for constitutional advice. *Les Marchands* of Caussade Market for feeding me. All of those at INRA Les Vigneres near Cavaillon who got me interested in France in the first place. Plus, all the other French people I've stayed with, drank with, eaten with and worked with over the years for their help and encouragement. Merci.

About Philip Ogley

Born in 1974, Philip Ogley grew up in Leeds. Since then he's lived and worked in many different countries as a holiday rep, barman, chef, writer, caretaker, bicycle courier, English teacher, labourer, Christmas tree seller, conservationist, waiter, driver, canoe instructor, bookseller, field researcher. He lives in France. This is his first novel.

www.pjogley.com

Liked the book?
Why not leave a review?
Thanks.

Printed in Great Britain
by Amazon